"Vicki, I Think You Know How You're Affecting Me."

His words, and the look of desire in his eyes, made her heart race doubletime with a wild mixture of fear and anticipation.

"But I've got to tell you before we get involved," he continued, "I'm not much into commitments." His lips were inches from her ear now and she felt his warm caress. "If you want me to stop, I will."

"I don't know," she whispered, frightened of her own response to this darkly handsome stranger.

"It has to be your decision," his voice told her, but his hands and lips spoke otherwise.

ALYSSA HOWARD

lives in Maryland and is a wife and mother as well as a writer. She loves writing romances because they celebrate the most joyful part of a woman's life—and there is always a happy ending.

D0273382

Dear Reader:

SILHOUETTE DESIRE is an exciting new line of contemporary romances from Silhouette Books. During the past year, many Silhouette readers have written in telling us what other types of stories they'd like to read from Silhouette, and we've kept these comments and suggestions in mind in developing SILHOUETTE DESIRE.

DESIREs feature all of the elements you like to see in a romance, plus a more sensual, provocative story. So if you want to experience all the excitement, passion and joy of falling in love, then SILHOUETTE DESIRE is for you.

I hope you enjoy this book and all the wonderful stories to come from SILHOUETTE DESIRE. I'd appreciate any thoughts you'd like to share with us on new SILHOUETTE DESIRE, and I invite you to write to us at the address below:

Meredith Morgan,
Silhouette Books,
320 Steelcase Rd., East,
Markham, Ontario
L3R 2M1

ALYSSA HOWARD
Southern Persuasion

 Silhouette Desire

Published by Silhouette Books New York

Distributed in Canada by PaperJacks Ltd., a Licensee
of the trademarks of Simon & Schuster, Inc.

Other Silhouette Books by Alyssa Howard

Love Is Elected

SILHOUETTE BOOKS, a Division of Simon & Schuster, Inc.
1230 Avenue of the Americas, New York, N.Y. 10020
In Canada distributed by PaperJacks Ltd.,
330 Steelcase Road, Markham, Ontario

Distributed by Pocket Books

ISBN: 0-671-47337-9

First Silhouette Books printing November, 1983

10 9 8 7 6 5 4 3 2 1

Printed in Canada

BC91

Southern
Persuasion

1

As she stood at the entrance surveying the ornate red and gold decor of the Airport Hotel's Palm Room, Victoria Johnson was unaware that several pairs of admiring male eyes had turned in her direction. The room was filled with businessmen and computer professionals looking for a chance to unwind at the end of a hectic conference. And a woman like Vicki with her tall, slim good looks and vibrant auburn hair, was definitely considered fair game—even with the cool, professional image she had taken pains to project.

Vicki glanced at the gold digital watch on her slender wrist and grimaced. It was already six-thirty. Where was Hank Bouchard, anyway? He'd spent a good half-hour lecturing her on the importance of showing up at this party. And now she was the only Montgomery Office Systems employee in sight.

"This West Coast exhibition is important to Montgomery's future," he'd repeated at least half a dozen times in the last two days since they'd brought their new word processing system down from Santa Barbara. "And you've got to milk every opportunity. You've done a great job giving demonstrations and answering questions. But the cocktail party this evening is your last chance to make an impression on these guys." Hank rubbed an impatient hand across the top of his balding head and shot Vicki a challenging look. "And you know how much Montgomery needs a big contract out of this conference."

Vicki's deep emerald eyes had narrowed. She did know how much Montgomery needed to make the first critical sales of their new system. But she also knew what Hank would never dare say. One of the reasons he considered her such an asset to the sales team was that her looks attracted customers. But, she assured herself, after they were interested, it was her computer knowhow that kept them listening.

Nevertheless, a month ago she would have refused point-blank to let Hank maneuver her into attending the cocktail party. Her change of heart could be attributed to her sister Sally's parting words last week.

"You've got to stop being such a recluse," her sister had lectured. "You're young and attractive. A pretty girl like you should be out dating every good-looking guy in sight instead of running the other way when a man gets within two feet of you."

"You're exaggerating," Vicky had protested. "You make me sound like a wallflower, and that's not true at all. I'm just selective."

Sally had snorted derisively. "Selective, that's for sure. To get through your screen a man has to combine the passive personality of a Caspar Milquetoast with the looks of Robert Redford and the brains of Henry Kissinger." Sally shook her head. "You know what I mean, Vicki. Promise me that while you're on this trip you'll get out and circulate and won't be so standoffish."

Vicki had reluctantly promised.

Yet, as she stood in the archway of the elegant Palm Room she couldn't help having a few second thoughts. For the past two years, she had made it a hard and fast rule never to socialize with male business associates. And it was difficult to break longstanding patterns.

Come on, Vicki, she told herself, smoothing out the fabric of her pale apricot silk shirtwaist. Sally's right. You can't stick your head in the sand forever. And if you're going to make any sales for Montgomery Systems at this convention, socializing is definitely part of the job description. Anyway, she added, you're here now. So you might as well give it your best shot—with or without Hank.

Looking around the room, Victoria spotted a likely group of company representatives and headed in their direction.

"Hi, I'm Vicki Johnson from Montgomery Systems," she began with a tentative smile. "Did you get a chance to stop by our booth in the exhibit hall?"

Six male heads turned in her direction and gave her an appreciative look.

"No, I didn't, honey," the portly, middle-aged conventioneer next to her said with a grin, as he draped a plaid sportcoat-clad arm around her slender shoulder. "But I sure wish I had."

The rest of the group guffawed, and Vicki decided to back off.

"We'll be glad to set up a demonstration for your office, if you give us a call," she offered, wriggling out from under the proprietary arm and handing one of the group a business card before backing away gracefully. This bunch must have started happy hour around noon, she thought. And they seemed as interested in talking about business as schoolboys playing truant. At least she felt she had handled the situation smoothly under the circumstances.

But as she turned to survey the room again, she suddenly met the amused glance of a rakish-looking stranger. His long, lean frame propped lazily against the bar, he was watching her closely, a faint smile on his firm, well-cut mouth. She wanted to turn away, but his devilish blue eyes held her captive for a long moment. Lifting up his glass in a toast, he winked and then took a swallow of his drink.

There was something vaguely familiar about his rugged features, sexy mustache, and wavy dark hair. Had he stopped by the Montgomery Systems booth during the conference? She didn't think so. Even though she wasn't actively looking for eligible men, surely she would remember anyone that devastatingly attractive. As he shifted his position, she couldn't help noticing the ripple of hard muscles under his expensive sportcoat, silk shirt, and crisp gabardine slacks.

Realizing that she was staring, Vicki quickly turned away. She was here to sell a system, not to go "ga ga" over some good-looking stranger. Shoulders squared and head held high, Victoria plunged once again into the milling crowd.

For the next twenty minutes she concentrated on making contacts, talking up the Montgomery word processing system, and giving out business cards. But none of the partygoers she approached seemed very interested in business. What did Hank think would come of this little foray, she asked herself in exasperation, fighting off the beginning of a headache. This was harder work than manning the Montgomery booth at the convention and a lot less profitable. Assignments like this made her wish she'd stayed in the purely technical side of data processing, like her engineer Barry. Hank hadn't insisted that *he* waste hours looking for new business prospects here.

Willing her exasperation not to show, Vicki looked around the room again. No sign of Hank. Where was that smooth operator anyway? She had done her duty to

Montgomery Systems, for whatever it was worth, but salesmanship in this type of situation wasn't her forte. Maybe she should just grab a bite to eat and go back upstairs.

After wending her way through the crowd toward the buffet table, she took a plate from the stack and began to make her selections. There was the usual assortment of cocktail party fare—Swedish meatballs, raw vegetables with dip, hot dogs in pastry, and an assortment of cheese and crackers.

Not much of a dinner, she mused, reaching over to spear two meatballs. It was just then that a waiter appeared with a hot tray of fragrantly spiced shrimp, which he set on the table directly in front of her.

What timing, she thought, scooping up several of the delectable morsels. But half the partygoers suddenly had the same idea. There was soon a press of bodies in back of her, all jockeying for position by the shrimp tray. As she tried to wiggle out of the throng, she felt an elbow jam into her ribs. And then something cold and wet splashed onto her back.

"Oops, pardon me," a red-faced man muttered before pushing on toward the shrimp.

Vicki was left to find her way out of the crowd.

Great, that's just what I needed, she thought with annoyance, trying to twist around and survey the damage. She could see a burgundy splotch on her back. It was red wine, and that meant a permanent stain if she didn't get it out fast.

She had edged over to the side of the room, trying to decide what to do, when a hand on her shoulder startled her into awareness of her surroundings again. It was the darkly handsome stranger who had been lounging at the bar.

"A lady in distress," he drawled, the tinge of a Southern accent in his deep voice. "Can I be of assistance?"

Vicki, her nerves already on edge from the accident, was about to issue a negative reply automatically. But the look of genuine concern on his ruggedly attractive face stopped her.

"If we get some cold water and salt on that stain right away, I think we can save your dress," he suggested.

"Do you really think so?"

"I've seen it done before," he assured. "Let me give it a try."

Grateful but still a bit wary, Vicki let herself be led over to a serving table near the back of the room, where she set down her plate of food.

"Now, hold still," the stranger commanded, dipping a cloth napkin into a pitcher of ice water and reaching for a salt shaker.

It was more than the coldness of the water that made her shiver as he began to rub industriously at the splotch, which started at the small of her back and ended just above her waistline. Something about the intimate way he steadied her waist with his strong left hand made her pulse quicken.

"Am I being too rough?" he inquired solicitously, his warm breath inches from her ear.

And then his hand was inside the back of her collar, pulling the fabric away from her body as he scrubbed at the stain.

Vicki flushed and started to twist away. "I think it's okay, and you needn't go to any more trouble," she stammered.

The stranger threw back his head and laughed. "No trouble—I'm between jobs so I might as well make myself useful somehow."

As he spoke, he withdrew his hand and stepped back.

"All done. And that silky material should dry quickly, so you won't catch your death of cold."

Now that the intimate contact was broken, Vicki found herself able to think more clearly again.

"Thank you for your help," she acknowledged. "It's a little hard to scrub your own back in a situation like this."

"My pleasure," he assured smoothly.

And Vicki found her cheeks begin to burn again.

"If you don't like being scrubbed by a perfect stranger, let me introduce myself. Clayton Harper at your service, ma'am. But call me Clay."

"Victoria Johnson," she replied automatically. She might have gone on to mention Montgomery Office Systems, but she had decided to quit for the evening. Anyway, this guy said he was out of work so he probably wasn't a potential customer, she rationalized. But the man was intriguing, she had to admit, studying his strong chiseled features and startling blue eyes. He had an air of easy charm about him that any woman would have found appealing. And for all her wary attitude toward men, Vicki was definitely woman enough to appreciate it. On the other hand, she wasn't prepared for his next question.

"Had enough of the party?" he asked, his eyes locking with hers for a moment.

Caught off balance, Vicki responded without thinking.

"Actually I'm exhausted. I'm ready to call it a night."

"I'm with you." His blue eyes took on a devilish glint. "How about joining me in a nightcap?"

Instantly, Vicki's guard was up, and yet there was something about the man that made her want to get to know him better. With anyone else she would have ended the conversation long before. But Clayton Harper, with his combination of startling good looks and Southern charm, interested her in a way few men had lately. However, his next words brought back her old defensiveness in force.

"How about coming up to the rooftop lounge for a drink?" he suggested, his voice lowering to an intimate tone. "I'd like to get better acquainted."

I'm sure you would, Vicki thought, shooting him a look

that told him she could read between the lines. Letting herself be picked up by a stranger, no matter how appealing, had never been her style. Yet she was still torn between his charm and her reservations.

It was only when she spotted Hank Bouchard strolling into the Palm Room that the issue was finally decided. If he caught her alone, she knew she would be in for another two hours of making the rounds. And that prospect was definitely depressing.

"Listen," she whispered to her companion. "I'm willing to make a deal. You pretend to be interested in buying a million dollars' worth of word processing equipment, and I'll have one drink with you."

"A million dollars' worth of equipment? That's a little high for one drink, isn't it—and for someone out of a job, too."

"I didn't say you had to buy, only sound as if you're interested when my manager comes over."

Hank had already spotted Vicki and started to thread his way across the room in her direction. "How are you doing?" he asked meaningfully.

"Uh, Clay here wants to hear some more about our new products," she told him. "We were just going to discuss them over a drink."

"Our forty-three district offices are going to put in word processing soon," Clay added for good measure. "And I'm very interested in what Vicki has to offer."

All smiles, Hank practically escorted them out of the room.

When her manager was out of sight, Vicki turned to Clay. "Wasn't that overdoing it a little bit?" she questioned.

But he only grinned. "Just following instructions," he pointed out, as he led her across the lobby. "I've got to make a quick stop at the desk. Why don't you get us an elevator?"

"Okay," Vicki agreed, and ten minutes later they were crossing the threshold of the Penthouse Bar. A crowd of people dressed for action, women in slinky jumpsuits and men with shirts open to the waist and gold chains bouncing on hairy chests, swayed to the piercing sound of a throbbing rock number. Vicki stopped dead and rolled her eyes in dismay. This place would surely turn her fledgling headache into a whopper. And headache or no, it would be impossible to hold a conversation over the din.

Clayton grimaced knowingly. Bending, he whispered in her ear, "Not your scene?"

Vicki shook her head emphatically, and Clay took her elbow and led her out into the corridor. The elevator door slid open, and a gaggle of merrymakers spilled out.

"Luck is with us," Clayton observed. "Let's make the most of it."

In the next moment he had propelled her into the empty elevator.

"Where are we going?" Vicki asked. The silence in the small intimate compartment was deafening after the noise and confusion of the Penthouse Bar. Suddenly she was vividly aware of being alone with a total stranger.

"To someplace quieter," he replied in a reassuring voice. Just then the elevator shuddered to a halt and the door shushed open. "Right down the hall," he directed, taking her arm once more and leading her into the carpeted hallway.

Suspicions were beginning to form in Vicki's mind.

"What's just down the hall?" she wanted to know.

Without answering, Clay stopped in front of a door and inserted a key in its lock. When the door swung open he made a sweeping gesture of welcome.

Vicki hesitated. "But this is your room. . . ." she began, taking a step backward.

"Come into my parlor," he intoned in a mock villainous voice, twirling his mustache in a melodramatic fashion.

Vicki gave him an assessing look. The mischievous glint in his blue eyes was her undoing. Yet her answering laugh had a slightly nervous edge as she followed him inside. For the first time in months, her own motives were unclear. But one thing she did know, at twenty-six years of age, she was big enough to take care of herself. What's more, she could leave any time things got out of hand, she rationalized as she moved across the plush beige carpeting.

Behind the anonymous hotel door was a comfortable sunken sitting area. Doors to the left and right undoubtedly led to bedrooms. And one window wall presented a magnificent view of the Los Angeles skyline.

"This must be a very expensive suite," Vicki observed, looking around. "Just how does an out-of-work computer type rate a setup like this?"

Clay grinned engagingly. "You know how it is when you register late at one of these conventions. You end up with either the laundry room or the palace. This time I lucked out with opulence. And I can offer you more than a drink."

At Vicki's raised eyebrow, he hurried on, "Let me get you some food. Remember, your plateful of goodies is still down in the Palm Room."

"You're right, a drink would do me in on an empty stomach," Vicki admitted, laying her evening bag on the table. Settling herself on one of the gray velvet modular couches, she watched Clay's curly dark head disappear behind the bar.

She wished she knew more about him. On the surface he seemed relaxed and casual. But she could sense an underlying current flowing between them that kept her from letting down her guard completely. Yet there was probably no other man who could have gotten her up to his room on such short acquaintance and with such a flimsy excuse, she admitted to herself. What was she doing here, really? If she were smart, she would leave right now. But somehow she couldn't force herself to take that easy out. Part of her wanted to find out what was going to happen and how she would handle it.

When Clay reemerged, he was holding a large tray full of tempting cheeses, crackers, pepperoni rounds, sliced vegetables, and marinated artichoke hearts.

"Looks like you were prepared for entertaining," Vicki observed. "You can go into competition with that party downstairs anytime."

Clay set the plate in front of her on the glass and chrome coffee table and grabbed a celery stick for himself as he turned back to the bar.

"Midnight snacks are my specialty," he acknowledged. "So I asked the management to keep this place well stocked. What would you like to drink?"

"How about a blackberry sour?" Vicki asked wickedly, assuming that he wouldn't have the necessary equipment or ingredients for such an unusual drink.

But Clayton was unfazed. "Coming right up," he sang out as he pulled out a bottle of blackberry brandy and placed a small blender on the bar.

Vicki ate a wedge of cheese as she watched Clay fix her frosty drink and then a bourbon on the rocks for himself.

"Have you been job hunting at the convention?" she asked.

"I've been looking into a few things," he answered noncommittally, sauntering across the room and setting the two drinks down on the table. His lips twitched in a faint smile. "You have to be prepared to take advantage of opportunities that come along," he added, as he sank down beside her on the soft cushions of the couch.

His closeness made Vicki's pulse quicken and the skin on the back of her arm tingle. And the tangy scent of his cologne was affecting her ability to concentrate. To hide her strong reaction to his electric presence, she reached over and picked up her drink.

"This is delicious," she acknowledged with pleasure, taking a sip of the fruit-flavored concoction. "It's more like a fruit freeze than a mixed drink. Did you work your way through college tending bar?"

"I've been many things professionally," he murmured. "But tending bar is strictly a hobby."

Jobs seemed like a relatively safe topic of conversation, Vicki decided, edging slightly away from Clay as she took another sip of her drink. But putting a few inches between them didn't lessen her awareness of his hard, muscular body.

"Exactly what type of professional experience do you have?" she inquired, trying to get her mind back on a more appropriate track.

He slanted her a mocking blue-eyed glance that told her he was well aware of her tactics. "My degree is in engineering, but I found out fast that the real challenges were in system design. I was part of the team that put together Voyager's computer guidance system. That was an experience I really enjoyed."

Vicki looked up at him with new respect. Everyone knew what an amazing job that group of programmers had done. "I'm impressed," she told him.

He shrugged off her compliment. "How did a nice girl like you get involved in this crazy business?" he questioned, directing the conversation away from his achievements.

"I was lucky. My high school math teacher steered me to computer science in the first place."

"So you're not just selling, then?" Clay asked, stretching his arm out on the sofa so that it brushed against the back of her neck in what seemed to be an unintentional contact. But even that light touch sent a quiver of awareness through her body. And she looked quickly down at her drink.

"That's right, I was in on the development of the system we've brought down here," she said, unable to stifle the touch of pride in her voice.

"So tell me about Montgomery," he prompted. "Supposing I had millions at my disposal. Why would I want to buy my office automation equipment from y'all?"

This was a topic that Vicki could warm to easily. And it gave her a chance to focus on something besides the undeniable sex appeal of her companion.

"Two years ago Montgomery was an established office equipment firm," she began. "But when Ellen Montgomery, my boss, took over the reins from her father, she knew that to stay on top she'd have to get into computers quickly."

For the next fifteen minutes Vicki enthusiastically filled him in on the firm's recent progress. And Clay listened with such apparent interest that she began to feel as though she were talking to a friend of long standing.

"Aren't you getting bored with all of this?" she finally asked.

But Clay shook his head. "Anything you have to say is fascinating," he drawled. "It's your combination of beauty and brains that I find so intriguing."

Vicki stiffened. Clay's casually spoken remark had put her on the alert again, like a deer who suddenly picks up the scent of a puma on the prowl.

Ever since she left college to work in a field dominated by men, her good looks had made her subject to constant sexual pressure from male colleagues and clients. In the beginning, she hadn't known how to cope with it. And her first boss had taken advantage of her uncertainty to exert a lot more pressure than she'd been ready to handle. Because of his harassment, that job had ended disastrously. At the time it had left her self-esteem perilously low and made her wary of all men who were attracted to her. And even though she was outwardly back on an even keel, there were scars that had yet to heal.

"You certainly have your lines well polished," she charged now. And there was no way Clay could fail to pick up the hostility in her voice.

Her host gave her an injured look. "It's not a line. I meant it as a compliment. But I've obviously touched a sore spot. What's the problem?"

Vicki turned her blackberry sour glass in her hand. Maybe she had overreacted this time. After all, tonight was just a case of ships passing in the night. When she looked up at Clay again, there was a forced smile on her lips that wasn't quite reflected in her eyes. "Just shell shock from the convention," she apologized. "I've been fielding clever lines all week."

"I'll bet," Clay agreed lightly, though inwardly he suspected there was more to her outburst than she was letting on.

For one long moment they sat in silence, each searching for something to say. Then Vicki lifted her glass to take a sip and noticed it was empty. "I guess I'm all out," she said.

"Let me get you another drink," he offered, standing up.

Vicki hesitated and then agreed. "Oh, why not?" Despite the ups and downs of their conversation, the drink she had just finished had finally begun to make her feel relaxed—and a little reckless.

As Clay stood at the bar mixing Vicki's second blackberry sour, he looked very much at ease. Yet his thoughts were anything but easy. Vicki was the most appealing woman he had met in a long time. Her fresh good looks had attracted him downstairs at that noisy cocktail party, and he had only been thinking about getting her into his bed then. But now, having talked to her, he was impressed by her brains and intrigued by her lively personality. And that had changed the picture. He was feeling strangely protective of this woman. He still wanted her, but his conscience dictated that he warn her about himself. Commitment wasn't something he could handle. He had convinced himself of that years ago and had never found a reason to change his mind. There were just too many good-looking women willing to take whatever he had to give. And he had always rationalized that it was better to keep the involvement short-term—so no woman would end up with the heartbreak his mother had endured in her marriage to the hard-driving workaholic Patrick Harper, who'd neglected his family and died of a heart attack in his prime. You're just like your father, too many business associates had told Clay. And deep down he was afraid it was true. Suddenly the old fear he constantly suppressed came knifing to the surface of his brain. And you're going to end up like him too, the inner voice he hated reechoed its foreboding assessment of his future.

Refusing to grapple with this familiar specter, Clay propelled himself into a well-practiced mode. There was only one sure way to banish that inner demon—by losing himself in the warm arms of a willing woman. Yet, he told himself, looking over at Vicki, I have to give her some warning. The cards had already been dealt in this game of theirs. But Vicki was clearly a novice blackjack player who didn't know he was dealing from a rigged deck. He didn't doubt the outcome, but his conscience insisted that if the game were to continue, he would have to show his own cards.

It took Clay only a few minutes to refill her glass with the exotic, icy cocktail. And while he worked deftly at the bar, Vicki studied his whipcord-lean body and handsome features, admitting again her attraction to this man.

Maybe Sally's right after all, she thought. Every guy I meet through my job doesn't have to be a threat. And besides, she added reassuringly, I'm not going to have to face Clay at the office Monday morning. So if he's not the kind of person he seems to be now, it won't matter so much. After all, we're not going to have an ongoing relationship.

Suddenly it came to Vicki that in a way she was using Clay Harper to find out something about herself. Was that fair, her conscience whispered. But the drink had made her more than just relaxed and reckless. It had swept away some of her usual qualms.

On his way back to the sofa, Clay turned on the stereo. The vibrant strains of a Mozart string quartet filled the room. Vicki sat sipping the drink, enjoying the music, and admiring the bird's-eye view of the Los Angeles skyline. The sun was beginning to set, and it tinged the tall buildings with amber fire. On one level, she enjoyed the view. But she was still very much aware of her companion and their perhaps too intimate environment. When she felt Clay's arm slip around her shoulder, she stiffened in the old reflex.

"Relax. Don't tense up on me," Clay whispered. "That villain stuff at the door was just an act." Vicki looked up into his vibrantly blue eyes. If she were honest with herself, she'd admit that she was more than curious to know what his kiss would be like.

As Clay read her expression, his fingers began to caress her shoulder lightly. The sensation sent an instant shiver of pleasure down her spine, and this time she did not draw away. Something about this man aroused her primitive needs and emotions.

"Vicki, I think you know how you're affecting me."

His words, and the look of desire in his eyes, made her heart rate double with a wild mixture of both fear and anticipation.

"But I've got to tell you before we get involved," he continued, "I'm not much into commitments." His lips were inches from her ear now, and she felt his warm breath caress. "But if you want me to stop, I will." However, he had already made that almost impossible for both of them now.

"I don't know," she whispered, a little frightened of her own response to this darkly attractive stranger.

"It has to be your decision," his voice told her, but his hands and lips spoke otherwise. Suddenly Vicki knew that this man wanted her now as much as she wanted him. The strong emotion was both disturbing and exciting at the same time.

Clay took her silence for assent. Gently he pulled her close to his lean, hard torso. She felt the sensual brush of his mustache against her face, and then his lips were on hers, creating their own havoc with her senses. Suddenly she felt powerless to rouse herself from his mesmerizing embrace. Her lips opened eagerly to the exciting pleasure of his kiss as his probing tongue explored the moist sweetness of her mouth, creating delicious sensations. And then his mouth began to roam, tracing a trail of fire across her face toward her earlobe.

No one had ever aroused her in quite this way. Clayton Harper was drawing a powerful, primitive heat from the very center of her being. And despite her usual inhibitions, she was no more able to hold herself back than the sun was able to keep from rising in the morning. She felt his warm hands caressing the skin of her back through the thin silk of her shirtdress, while his lips moved down to nibble at the sensitive spot where her neck and shoulder joined. Throwing her head back, she enjoyed his explorations, while her own hands charted a trail of their own across his broad back before reaching up to tangle themselves in the thickness of his dark hair.

"Mmm, Vicki, that feels wonderful," he murmured. As

he spoke, his fingers found the buttons of her dress and began to slide them open. She heard him sigh with satisfaction when they yielded to his practiced onslaught.

Was she really allowing an almost total stranger to do this, one part of Vicki's mind wondered, as she felt him snap open the catch at the front of her lacy wisp of a bra. But the tiny voice was quickly silenced by the tide of heated sensations that swept over her. As his strong hands caressed the fullness of her breasts, she moaned and arched her back against him. Lifting her breasts in his cupped hands, he grazed their hardening nipples with his lips and then buried his face in the soft valley between them, his mustache an added stimulus to the heightened sensitivity of her skin.

For Vicki, the intense pleasure was almost unbearable. It had been so long since a man had caressed her in this way, and she wasn't prepared for the unquenchable excitement that flooded her body. She might have been a wax candle melting under the heated touch of this man. Without protesting she let Clay slip the shirtdress and bra from her shoulders as he trailed kisses on the creamy skin he uncovered.

Then she felt his lips against her ear and his urgent, passion-filled whisper. "Vicki, unbutton my shirt. I've got to feel you against my skin."

Her hands fumbled to do his bidding, but her own desire had made her fingers clumsy, and it seemed to take forever. Finally she pulled the shirtfront open and pushed the crisp material away from his shoulders. Quickly he freed his arms from the sleeves, and they were both naked to the waist.

He pushed her back onto the soft cushions of the sofa and his body covered hers. The touch of his hair-roughened chest against hers was almost too much to bear. Her breath was coming in ragged little gasps now, and she couldn't tell whether it was her own heart or his that she felt thumping so violently. Through the soft fabric of her dress, Vicki sensed the urgency of his male arousal and, instinctively, thrust her hips upward against his. Clay's response was a deep, shuddering sigh, and then his hands were at her waist, feeling for a belt buckle.

"How do you get this damn thing off?" he muttered, his voice thick with desire.

But before Vicki could direct him to the skirt's hidden pocket closure, the phone rang. Clay cursed. "I told them to hold all calls—except one. But I was hoping for better timing. I'll be right back." And suddenly Vicki was alone on the couch.

Sitting up, she looked around dazedly. She knew what would have happened if the phone hadn't interrupted them. And the thought made her cheeks flame. Hastily she slipped back into her bra, pulled up the front of her dress, and with shaky fingers refastened the buttons. Springing off the sofa as though it were hot, she crossed the room to the large mirror hanging there and began to straighten her clothes without really seeing her reflection. What in the world could she have been thinking of? Well, obviously she hadn't been using her head at all.

It was just then that Clay reappeared in the doorway, a broad smile on his face. "That's good news!" he announced. "I'm no longer unemployed."

"I'm glad for you," she said with sincerity, but also with a definite tremble in her voice. It was taking all her efforts to bring her tangled emotions under control. "And I'm also glad the call came when it did. I'm really not used to this lightning progress in getting acquainted."

Clay slipped a hand into his trouser pocket and leaned comfortably against the door frame. Obviously this scene was far less traumatic for him than it was for her. "Is there anything I can do to change your mind?"

Vicki shook her head. "You're not going to get the chance. But when you decide to buy your million dollars' worth of Montgomery Systems word processing equipment, you can have me come and set it up for you."

Clay laughed. "I may just do that."

Before he could say anything else, Vicki snatched her evening bag off the table and hurried out of the penthouse suite to the elevator.

2

*S*ally advised you to be a little more approachable, Victoria Johnson, not jump into bed with the first engineer who makes a pass, Vicki scolded herself as she emerged from the elevator on the fourth floor.

To be honest, she couldn't lay the blame for tonight on Clay alone. She had been testing her ability to cope with a male–female relationship. That, coupled with the instant attraction that flowed like an open current between them from the first touch, had been her undoing. She had forgotten her usual caution where men were concerned, and she could still feel a tingling awareness recalling the sensations his caressing fingers had evoked.

Thank goodness this convention was over and she wouldn't be running into Clayton Harper again, she told herself, striving to put real conviction into the thought. Yet a part of her didn't want to be convinced. She had been drawn to the man—like lightning to water. And she'd come very close to getting seared.

It had been his rakishly attractive looks and disarming good humor that had led her to cast her reservations aside and leave the party with him. But by the time he'd maneuvered her into his suite, she should have followed her first inclination and just left. She had foolishly believed she could handle him. But that was before she discovered how potent his lovemaking could be. Once he'd started touching her with his hands and lips, she hadn't wanted him to stop. Just the memory of his kisses, his caresses, and his naked skin still made her pulse throb like a jungle drum.

Vicki was glad the red-carpeted corridor leading to her room was empty. Heaven knows what I look like, she thought as she fumbled in her evening bag for her room key. A glance in the bathroom mirror confirmed her worst suspicions. Her thick, shoulder-length, auburn hair was a mass of unruly waves, and her usually calm green eyes gleamed with feverish brightness. But a splash of cold tap water across her face brought back a measure of composure.

She had just brushed out her hair and slipped into a sheer beige nightshift edged with lace when the phone next to the bed rang. Instinctively her hand reached out to pick up the receiver and then stopped in mid-air. It could only be one of two people, Hank Bouchard or Clay Harper, and she didn't want to talk to either one of them. Hank would want to know how her sales pitch had gone, and she certainly wasn't prepared to give a detailed account of tonight's activities. And what if Clayton Harper wanted to persuade her back to his suite? She wasn't ready to cope with that alternative either. She was still too susceptible to his brand of Southern persuasion to take a chance on letting him have another try.

She watched the phone, resisting the urge to pick it up, and counted fifteen rings before the persistent caller gave up. With a sigh of relief—but also a tinge of regret—Vicki turned off the bedside lamp and pulled the covers around her shoulders. Usually after a tiring day she could get to sleep almost at once. But not tonight.

Although she tried to relax, her body was still aroused by her encounter with Clay. At first she tried to lie very still, making her mind a blank, but it was no use. Thoughts of Clay's lovemaking kept rising to the surface of her mind like silver bubbles in a glass of champagne. With all her strength of will she tried to sweep them away—with no success. For a long time she lay rigid under the covers, aware of the contact of the sheets against her fevered skin. And then, finally, with trembling fingers she ran her hand down her body, delicately tracing, through the wispy nightshift, the places that Clay had touched. She could almost imagine that he was there with her, urging her to find out something about herself that she had kept long buried.

Suddenly she clenched her fists, aware of what she was doing. She might be frustrated, but she was damned if she was going to let Clay Harper have this effect on her. Resolutely she threw back the covers and climbed out of bed. Crossing to the thermostat she flipped on the air conditioning. Soon a blast of cold air brought her back to reality. Shivering, she crawled back under the covers.

Her last thoughts before she finally drifted off into a troubled sleep were of a dark stranger tipping his glass to her in a mock toast.

Luckily there was little time the next morning to think about Clayton Harper. Vicki had to pack her suitcase and meet Barry Carter, Montgomery's ace engineer. Together they were responsible for making sure all the Montgomery Systems equipment was properly crated. Vicki and Barry had put in a good three hours before they joined Hank at the registration desk for their ride back to Santa Barbara.

"Let's grab some breakfast on the highway," Hank suggested.

"Count me out on any food," Barry told him. "I had a

lulu of a night on the town, and after the kind of morning we just put in, all I want to do is sleep in the back seat."

Vicki looked sympathetically at her lanky engineer. She'd been wondering all morning why his bearded face lacked its usual sparkle of humor and his eyes were a tad bloodshot.

"Looks like you *could* use some beauty sleep," she teased. "But what I need is a good cup of coffee."

Once they were settled in the car, Barry was true to his word. Before they had turned off onto the freeway, he was already snoring loudly. Hank nodded toward the back seat and grinned. "Aren't you glad we didn't bring him along for conversation?"

Vicki had to laugh. "I'd say this was the only time Barry had been quiet all week—if he weren't snoring so loudly," she added.

"Maybe we can drown him out with some soothing rock and roll," Hank observed wryly, reaching for the radio knob and finding an appropriate station.

"Always the optimist," Vicki chuckled.

There was something so unthreatening about Hank, with his bald pate and rotund form, that Vicki could enjoy a type of casual banter with him that she couldn't share with her other male co-workers. Barry, too, was one of her few male friends at work. Even though he often teased her, she knew he was devoted to his wife Bonnie. Relaxing back against her seat, she looked out the car window. The morning was typical for a Southern California spring, with gray smog hiding the sun.

"I'd take the Coast Highway," Hank remarked, "since I know you like to look at the ocean. But you won't be able to see it anyway, so we might as well opt for the fast route."

Vicki shot him a knowing glance. "You were going that way anyway, weren't you?" she commented wryly. "But now you don't have to feel guilty about it."

They were still in the San Fernando Valley when Hank pulled into the large parking lot of a pancake house.

"I guess this place specializes in handling big appetites, if that colossus there is any indication," Vicki observed, pointing toward the restaurant entrance, where a twenty-five-foot statue of a pot-bellied monk held a six-foot platter of pancakes.

Hank looked at the figure and shook his head. "That's the thing I love about this area. Everyone's in the entertainment business."

"Shall we wake up Barry?" Vicki questioned.

"No. Let's take him at his word," Hank suggested, closing the door carefully so as not to disturb the sleeping engineer.

Inside the restaurant, a hostess dressed like Maid Marian showed them to a cheerful window booth. After scanning the menu, Hank ordered a stack of pancakes, and Vicki settled on an omelette with mushrooms and Gruyere cheese.

"Well," he asked, as the waitress poured them each a cup of hot coffee, "how did you do with C. L. Harper last night?"

"C. L. Harper," she repeated blankly. "Where would I have met C. L. Harper, the wonder boy of the computer industry?" The words were barely out of her mouth when the realization dawned. "Surely you don't mean Clayton? He isn't . . . he couldn't . . ."

Hank chuckled knowingly. "Don't play dumb with me, Vicki. I was there when the two of you walked out of the party as thick as thieves. I hope you made the most of that opportunity to extol the virtues of Montgomery's new systems."

Vicki bent her head, pretending to be completely absorbed with stirring cream and sugar into her coffee. How could she have been so blind, she railed at herself. So that's why Clay's handsome features had seemed familiar. And he hadn't even bothered to hide his name. How could I have not recognized him?

A look of anger crossed her face as another thought surfaced. Out of a job, my foot! He must have been laughing at me all the time, she fumed. Well, I'm certainly not going to let Hank get a laugh out of this, too.

"Um, I don't think Mr. Harper was really interested in our word processing equipment," she hedged. "Although he certainly pretended to be at the beginning of our, uh, conversation."

Hank gave her a speculative look. "Come on, Vicki," he chided lifting a bushy eyebrow. "I've never known the man who could get the better of you. If he was playing games, you must have been right in there batting yourself." And then inspiration struck. Leaning back in his chair, Hank smiled broadly. "I've just figured it out," he announced with satisfaction. "Clever as you are, you'd had enough of the cocktail party and used Harper as an excuse to get away. Am I right?"

Vicki cleared her throat. "You really can see right through me, Hank. But, you know, it wasn't fair leaving me to the wolves," she added, warming to the ready-made explanation. "If you want me to stay at one of those things next time," she justified, "come and do half the work."

Hank held up his hand. "Okay, okay, you win. The next time I get stuck in the cocktail lounge with a sure prospect, I'll send you a message."

"How did you do?" Vicki asked absently.

"Dead end," Hank acknowledged with a sigh. A sly grin began to twitch at the corners of his lips. "What about you and Harper?" he asked. "I've heard he's really got a technique with the ladies."

Vicki's eyebrows snapped together. "Let's just say that I was an opportunity Mr. Harper failed to capitalize on and leave it at that."

The sharp edge to her voice warned Hank not to push the subject. With resolution Vicki tried to shove her angry thoughts about Clayton Harper to the back of her mind. For the rest of the meal they talked about how Montgomery Systems had been received at the convention and the reports they would each be filing with their boss. The thought of their lively company president brought a smile to Vicki's face.

Two years ago she had come to work for Ellen Montgomery after leaving her first job—the one that had ended so disastrously. After her stormy resignation, she had been unemployed for three months before finding a position at Montgomery Systems. The new association had worked out fine, and now Vicki looked forward to delivering Ellen a favorable report. What's more, Montgomery's success was important—and not only because Vicki wanted to please her boss. There could be personal gain as well. When she'd taken the job with the fledgling company, she'd agreed to start with a smaller base salary, which Ellen had supplemented with company stock. Vicki was determined that her efforts would make that stock worth something someday soon.

In less than an hour Hank's car was back on the highway heading for Santa Barbara. As they rode, Vicki looked out the window, remembering the time not so long ago when the roadside view had been mostly yellow hills and live oak trees. Now an endless succession of subdivisions, shopping centers, and the like lined the highway. And the area had certainly lost its appeal in the transition from ranchland to urban sprawl, she concluded.

But as the car climbed the pass toward Camarillo, her spirits picked up. The long grade had always held a special significance for her. She knew that on the other side she'd soon see the limitless expanse of the Pacific

Ocean spread out at the feet of the sturdy coastal mountains. As an added bonus, the sun was shining on the other side of the pass. Vicki felt her mood brighten even more.

When they reached the Santa Barbara city limits, she turned toward the back seat. "Time to rise and shine," she sang out in a loud voice.

Barry stretched. "That's the kind of trip I like," he informed his colleagues in the front seat. "Over before you know it."

After they had stopped at Barry's neatly kept bunga-low near the beach, Vicki looked over at Hank. "Would you mind letting me off at my sister's house?" she asked. "I promised to stop by for a visit on the way home."

"Glad to oblige," Hank assured her, heading down State Street toward the rambling mission-style house where Sally and her husband Jeff resided with their two children, Beth and Matthew. Vicki had lived with them before getting her own place in one of the city's many apartment developments, but the closely knit family was still very much a part of her life.

As Hank pulled into the circular drive, Vicki looked around at the orange, lemon, and tangerine trees gracing the wide lawn. Their tangy fragrance was a welcome greeting. Before the car had even stopped in front of the white stucco house with its traditional red-tile roof, the paneled front door flew open. Out bounded six-year-old Matthew followed closely by four-year-old Beth.

"It's Aunt Vicki," the boy cried, racing forward with arms spread wide.

Alighting from the car, Vicki bent down to receive two sticky hugs. "Someone's been eating peanut butter and jelly," she guessed as she inspected the damage to her outfit. Luckily she was wearing jeans and a Western shirt—all washable.

Vicki looked up to meet the amused glance of her

sister. The two young women bore a strong family resemblance. But Sally's lighter hair was cut in the more conservative style of a young matron, and her blue jean–clad figure was a bit fuller after eight years of marriage and two children. "I don't know whether to give you a hug or a wet paper towel," she laughed, sending the kids off to wash their hands.

After Hank left, the two young women made their way through the cool interior of the house, furnished in traditional Spanish hacienda style with red terrazzo floors, Indian rugs, and sturdy oak furniture. Sally pushed open the door to the covered patio at the back overlooking the heated swimming pool.

"As you might guess, Jeff is with a client; but he'll be back in time for dinner," she explained.

Vicki nodded. She knew how much Jeff was wrapped up in his insurance business right now.

Just then the youngsters reappeared and made another beeline for their Aunt Vicki. "What did you bring us from Los Angeles?" Matthew demanded.

"Now, really," Sally scolded. "Is that the only reason you want to see your aunt?"

Both children looked guiltily at their sneakers. But Vicki only grinned and reached into her purse to pull out an assortment of convention promotion giveaways. The children were delighted with the magic cube key chains, decks of trick cards, and fuzzy notebook stick-ons.

"I made them give me two of everything," she explained.

The kids sat down to play contentedly with their loot, and Sally turned to her sister. The two of them had always been close, and after their parents had died in a boating accident off Catalina Island, it had seemed only natural for Sally to invite the then-teenaged Vicki to live with her and her new husband, Jeff. Vicki had worried at first that the arrangement might be awkward. But she had fit right into the household and had been an enormous help to her sister when Matt was born the next year.

Her relationship with Jeff had been great, too. He'd encouraged her interest in computers and sent her to one of the best computer science programs in the country at Stanford. He'd even loaned her the money for her education, though their own financial situation was tight. That was one of the reasons why she'd been so anxious to keep her first job, despite the sexual pressures to which her boss, Jerry Pratt, had subjected her—to pay Jeff and Sally back. However, when Jerry's persistent attempts to maneuver her into his bed had become too blatant to ignore, Vicki had finally marched away from her job, vowing never to let another man harass her that way again. During the difficult time when she'd been pounding the pavement, trying to find exactly the right kind of new job, Sally had given her understanding and encouragement. Even during the bleak time when Vicki wondered if she'd ever get back on her feet, her sister had never lost faith. I'm lucky to have this kind of family, Vicki told herself, giving Sally a special smile.

"I'm glad you could stop off before going home. We don't get to see enough of you anymore," her sister complained.

Vicki nodded. "I know. It's just that we've all been so busy lately with the new line."

Sally shook her head. "Don't forget the old saw about all work and no play," she admonished. "You need to date more. Jeff said they've hired a new insurance underwriter at the main office. If you're interested . . ."

Vicki gave her sister a "you'll never give up" look, but Sally ignored it.

"Well, did you meet anybody interesting at the convention?"

"I thought I had," Vicki responded, gazing off toward the swimming pool and the jacaranda tree beyond. For a moment the clear blue water of the pool reminded her of the devilish blue glint in Clayton Harper's eyes as he bent down purposefully to take sensual possession of her lips. She felt herself quiver slightly in imagined response. Get a hold of yourself, Victoria, she scolded. With determination, she pushed the upsetting recollection out of her mind. "But I found out I'd made a mistake," she insisted firmly.

"Want to talk about it?" her sister asked sympathetically.

Vicki shook her head, unable to stop the telltale flood of color to her cheeks. "I think I'll just file this one away under 'learning experiences.' "

Knowing when to drop a sensitive subject, Sally steered the conversation to the Fiesta Committee she was chairing. "Beth is so excited. She's going to be a flower girl for the first time this year," she explained.

After that the talk turned naturally to the children. It was a pleasant change from the hectic activity of the convention, and Vicki found herself enjoying the visit even more than she'd anticipated.

As it turned out, her afternoon of chatting with Sally and playing with her niece and nephew was Vicki's last peaceful interlude for the next few weeks. After the unveiling of their new product, inquiries began to pour into Montgomery Office Systems, and Vicki was busy giving demonstrations and answering questions. But she was glad for the feverish activity as it left her little time to dwell on her devastating encounter with Clayton Harper. She congratulated herself on being able to push his darkly attractive features out of her mind—that is, until the April issue of *Computer Universe* crossed her desk. As she opened to the profile section, she was startled to lock eyes with his confident image gracing an in-depth interview. She wanted to slam the magazine shut, but some masochistic impulse made her read every word about his jet-propelled rise to success in the computer industry.

He had started with a NASA contract and then put together the small company that developed the game chip for Alien Invaders. Over the last ten years the thirty-five-year-old engineer had owned, built to success, and then resold a whole string of companies. The article compared Clay to his father, Patrick T. Harper, who had made quite a name for himself in the hi-fi business before dying ten years ago at the age of forty-five. The story then went on to speculate about Clay's financial holdings. Although he had amassed a small fortune, his straightforward responses to the interviewer's pointed questions made it clear that the challenge of each new conquest, not money, was his real motivation.

So that's why he told me he was between jobs, Vicki mused caustically. His good news probably meant another successful deal. It was obvious from her brief interlude, one part of her brain argued, that he treated women the same way—as challenges to be enjoyed for the moment before seeking new ones. He'd even mumbled something about not making long-term commitments. Yet the warmth and charm he had showed her belied that judgment. Had it just been an act?

Vicki turned to the end of the article, wondering if it mentioned his new job. But it had obviously been written before he was willing to talk about that particular deal.

Examining his picture again, she noted perversely that he looked even more attractive in person now that he sported a rakish mustache. That must have been why she hadn't recognized him. However, after her intimate encounter with Clayton Harper, there was no way that she would ever forget that face—mustache or no.

Her thoughts were interrupted by the beep of the computer terminal on her desk. The office's electronic mail system was delivering her a message. "Conference in my office in five minutes," the screen flashed a terse announcement from Ellen Montgomery.

What could be so urgent, she wondered, pushing back her chair. And who else was coming? Ellen hadn't even told her what to bring. That wasn't like her meticulous employer.

When Vicki entered the large corner office, several managers, Hank, and Barry were already seated around the wooden conference table. When she looked questioningly into Ellen's sparkling brown eyes, she could see her boss was about to burst with excitement. Pushing a lock of salt-and-pepper hair impatiently back from her forehead, the chicly dressed company president gestured toward an empty place near the head of the table. After Vicki seated herself, Ellen began.

"I've called you all together to announce our first big word processing contract," she bubbled. "It's with Data Dynamics International in Georgia. They want us to set up a three-month demonstration system at Stone Mountain Center near Atlanta. And there's promise of bigger things to come if all goes well."

"Great!" Hank boomed, rubbing his hands together. "Isn't Stone Mountain Center that new city-of-the-future enterprise that's supposed to open this summer?"

"Yes," Ellen confirmed. "The high technology computer industry leaders and the university research departments have teamed up to offer a unique living, working, and learning environment. I'm delighted that we've been selected to participate."

"How did we land this one?" Hank inquired.

"It must have been the fabulous job the three of you did at that L.A. show," Ellen returned, including Barry and Vicki in her praise.

Hank looked puzzled. "But I don't remember talking to anyone from DDI."

"And I was strictly behind the scenes," Barry added.

"Well, then, it must have been Vicki. One of the

specifications of the contract is that she comes along to oversee the project."

"What?" the young woman questioned in confusion. "I don't remember anyone from DDI either."

"Don't worry about it," Hank chortled. "They obviously remember you!"

Vicki had little time to ponder the mystery. The meeting became an impromptu planning session for the DDI contract. Barry and a crew of technicians would be joining Vicki at Stone Mountain, and he, Hank, and Vicki were kept busy answering questions all afternoon.

After that, the pace never slackened. If the few weeks before the L.A. conference had been busy, the next few were frantic. It seemed as if Vicki had to put in twenty-six hours a day preparing for the new assignment. She spent hours on the phone talking to the DDI contracting officer, picking a staff of technicians to accompany her, and making sure she understood the Montgomery word processing system inside out.

"I'll bet I could program this stuff in my sleep," she told Sally and Jeff at the bon voyage dinner they'd arranged for her.

"I'd be happier if you'd gotten more sleep in the last few days," her sister responded with concern in her voice.

But Jeff only laughed appreciatively at her observation. "I have every confidence in you, Vicki," he reassured her.

But the young woman herself had a few doubts. She remembered Ellen's last words just that afternoon.

"After you pull this off, it's going to be smooth sailing for Montgomery. I don't want to alarm you, but as a stockholder you ought to know that we've been in real need of capital for the past few months. But if this test goes well, the follow-up contract will put us in the black."

Vicki had given her a surprised look. She hadn't

known exactly how critical things were. What if she couldn't pull off the project and win the multi-million-dollar contract for Montgomery? It was such a big responsibility. And why had DDI insisted on her, she wondered. Instead of smooth sailing, might there be rocky shoals ahead at Stone Mountain Center?

3

Vicki pressed her forehead against the small window of the DC 727 now circling over Atlanta, preparing to land. Through the sparse layer of white clouds, she could see snatches of what she guessed was the downtown section of the city. The last few weeks had been so hectic that she'd hardly spared a thought for the Southern setting of her temporary assignment. But just before Vicki left, Ellen had given her a package of travel brochures and write-ups on Atlanta and the Stone Mountain Center. As she flipped through them while sipping a cup of airline coffee, her interest began to grow.

The new Stone Mountain Center was being sponsored by both national and international concerns. This opening summer alone, they expected two thousand permanent residents as well as fifty thousand tourists. The center's university would be offering seminars from top-name professors and well-known experts in the high technology fields. And there would be a wide variety of cultural and athletic activities as well.

What an opportunity, she thought. If everything goes smoothly with this demonstration project, I just may have time to enjoy myself.

But her work would have to come first. She knew now how much Ellen and the company were depending on her. And as a stockholder she had a personal stake in this as well. Montgomery really needed the large contract DDI was dangling in front of them. To get it, she'd have to convince their management that they needed Montgomery's system. Well, the equipment was superior; she knew that. But it would be her job to make sure everything went as planned. For a moment she let her mind wander back to a question that had been nagging her for the past few weeks. Why had DDI specifically asked for her? She still had no idea. But it really didn't matter. She was prepared to do whatever it took to bring the contract in.

Half an hour later, Vicki was standing at the baggage carousel waiting for her four pieces of luggage. As the stack of green leather suitcases materialized out of the rubber curtain, she heard a masculine voice with a pronounced Southern twang inquire politely, "Miss Johnson?" Turning quickly, she found herself looking at a pleasant, sandy-haired man in a pale blue business suit. She smiled her acknowledgment and identified herself.

"I'm Sam Woodhouse from DDI," said the affable young man. "I'm here to take you over to the Stone Mountain office. I'll see that your luggage is delivered to the house."

House, Vicki asked herself; surely he meant hotel. But before she could question him, he had taken her arm and called a porter to load her luggage. Then Vicki was being shepherded out the large glass doors into the balmy April air of Atlanta.

"It's been unusually warm this spring," Sam commented, making pleasant conversation as he helped Vicki into the plush, air-conditioned interior of a luxurious sleek, black car. Settling back into the comfort of its red leather upholstery, Vicki looked out the window with interest as Sam expertly maneuvered the car through the airport's heavy traffic and headed north on the expressway.

"What do you do for Data Dynamics?" she asked the young man beside her.

"I'm a personnel liaison," he explained. "We make sure things run smoothly so that people are comfortable."

"Big companies do seem to have all the amenities," Vicki acknowledged. "And so far I'm enjoying being taken care of so well."

The hour's drive to Stone Mountain took them through the city, past the Atlanta Braves stadium and the downtown skyscrapers.

"I never realized Atlanta was so modern," Vicki observed.

Sam laughed. "A lot of progress was made since the city was burned in the War Between the States."

Vicki nodded. "You've got me there. I *was* thinking of that scene in *Gone With the Wind.*"

As they continued on, Sam pointed out various landmarks. "The gold on the capital dome was mined in Daloniga, Georgia, and that revolving blue sphere is really a restaurant topping the Hyatt Regency."

"You're quite a good tour guide," Vicki complimented.

"I should be. I've been making this drive with new arrivals two or three times a week for months now," he informed her. "So if there's anything you want to know about the area, just ask."

As they approached the center's entrance, Vicki pulled a sheaf of papers from her briefcase and began reviewing some of her notes on DDI. First impressions were important, and she wanted to make sure she came across to her client favorably.

Satisfied with her quick review, Vicki looked up to her first view of Stone Mountain. "I had no idea it was that large!" she exclaimed.

Sam just laughed. "Most visitors are surprised by that mass of granite. But only a seventh of it is actually above ground. Be sure and go over to the park when you have time. There's a lot of Georgia history associated with this area."

Vicki made a mental note to do just that. By this time the car had slowed to a crawl.

"Can't make much headway around here now," Sam explained. "Everybody is too busy trying to cram three or four weeks' work into the last few days."

Vicki could see his point. All around people and equipment were in frantic motion—almost as though they were part of a movie being shown in fast forward. Up ahead, near the side of the road, was a huge flatbed truck loaded with what looked like hundreds of pots of geraniums. Even as it pulled to a halt, a squad of men began to unload the flowers while others stood by with trowels and shovels. Nearby a dozen painters were putting the finishing touches on a row of garden apart-ments. And another crew was laying sod beside a modernistic structure that Sam identified as the library.

"They've been working day and night to have things ready for the official opening next week," Sam informed her as he swung into a parking lot behind a large trailer. "These are the quarters we'll be operating from until we move into the permanent offices," he said as he opened Vicki's door.

Swinging her long legs out onto the gravel, Vicki smoothed the skirt of her pale green linen suit and stood up. The heels of her Italian bone-colored kid shoes immediately sank into the crushed stone.

"It's still a little primitive out here," Sam chuckled as he took her arm to help her right herself. "But it's pretty exciting, even with all the mud and construction. And when we move into the DDI complex, it's going to be positively plush."

"I'll take your word for it," Vicki acknowledged with a smile as she followed him inside. The interior of the temporary quarters was quite plush already, she noted with surprise, taking in the wood-grained paneling, comfortable couches in the reception area, and thick blue carpeting under her feet. She followed Sam down a long corridor, with small offices on either side, where clerical workers were busy typing away at computer terminals. The door at the end of the hall was marked "DDI Special Operations Center."

Ushering Vicki through, Sam leaned over the desk of the pretty young secretary. "Is the big boss in?" he asked jovially of the brown-eyed girl in the yellow shirtwaist dress. "I've brought Miss Johnson of Montgomery Systems to meet him."

The girl smiled a pleasant greeting. "You can take Miss Johnson right through."

"Thanks, Anita," Sam tossed over his shoulder as he pushed open the door to the inner office.

Vicki got a quick impression of a very masculine room dominated by a huge desk and decorated in earth tones. The "big boss," as Sam had styled him, was too engrossed to turn around at the moment. Head bent over and phone held firmly between shoulder and cheek, he was studying a set of architectural drawings and barking orders into the mouthpiece. But Vicki stiffened as she took in the voice and the long, lean masculine figure in shirtsleeves.

Oh no, her mind cried out in shocked denial. It couldn't be. But it was.

Conversation over, the boss hung up the phone and raised his eyes expectantly. There was no mistaking that rakish face. Vicki stared at the slightly arrogant tilt of his nose, the thick riverboat-gambler mustache, the sparkling blue eyes, and her heart sank into her stomach. It was Clay Harper, the man with whom she had made a fool of herself in Los Angeles last month.

Vicki stood rooted to the spot. Her mind was a whirl of disjointed and upsetting memories. How had this happened? How could Clay Harper be sitting in the vice-president's chair of DDI? But then, she recalled with a grimace, there was no question that Clay was a fast worker; witness the scene in his penthouse apartment. She remembered vividly how close she had come to surrendering to the persuasion of his exploring hands and probing tongue. Even now, watching his tanned, long-fingered hand still curled around the telephone receiver, she could almost feel his touch on her breast. And he was going to be her boss.

She'd spent a month exorcising C. L. Harper from her mind. Now, with a peculiar twist of fate, all her efforts were wasted. She could feel the tug of his magnetism all the way across the room, even as she seethed with anger at this situation. Oh yes, she was still attracted to him, Vicki admitted grudgingly to herself. But if he was trying to manipulate her the way Jerry Pratt had two years ago, he'd be in for a surprise. She had learned to take care of herself. The thought gave her courage, and a look of defiance glowed from her eyes.

As Clay's eyes took her in, a slow smile spread across his handsome features. "Well, well, Miss Johnson. We've been looking forward to having you down here. It's going to be a pleasure working with you," he drawled.

Vicki's eyes narrowed, and she stared at him hard. His smug satisfaction confirmed it. He'd been expecting her after all. There was no sign of surprise on his face, no sign of the shock she'd experienced. What kind of low-down game was he playing? She eyed him suspiciously.

"I didn't expect to see you here," she challenged.

Disregarding her comment, Clay turned to the young man at her side. "Thanks, Sam. Have Miss Johnson's

luggage transferred to her room. I'll see you this afternoon.''

Vicki struggled to maintain her composure as she
watched Sam leave. But her thoughts were in turmoil.

How naive she'd been that evening, she realized,
believing that she was using Clay Harper. She had
thought that because she would never see him again she
could find out something about herself through their brief
encounter. But now here he was, apparently all ready to
take up where they'd left off on the sofa.

Her first impulse was to turn on her heels and catch a
cab right back to the airport, but then she remembered
Montgomery Systems. Not only was this contract important to the company, she owed a personal debt to Ellen
for giving her a chance to prove her capability. For the
company's sake, and Ellen's sake too, she'd have to
hang around until she found out what was going on.
Besides, part of her now wanted to make Mr. Harper
sorry that he'd ever put her in this compromising position.

To judge from the amused expression forming on Clay
Harper's well-shaped lips, he knew exactly what effect
the situation was having on her. How could she maintain
a professional demeanor when his eyes were making a
leisurely inspection of her face and body? It was a major
effort of will for Vicki to meet his gaze squarely. But to her
surprise, Clay was quite direct when he began to speak.

"Won't you have a seat, Miss Johnson?" he said
gesturing at a plush barrel-shaped chair facing his desk.
Then, as they both sat down, Clay leaned back in his
swivel chair and remarked easily, "If you're wondering
about the coincidence in our meeting again, I might as
well admit that it's no coincidence at all. I asked for you
specifically as soon as I accepted DDI's offer of a vice-
presidency. You did sell me on Montgomery's equipment, you know, and I was impressed by your knowledge and your technical competence.'' He smiled

sardonically. "And I remember how well you handled yourself in difficult situations."

He paused, letting the remark sink in. Vicki shifted uncomfortably in her seat. What did he mean by that, she asked herself, or did she already know? Back in his penthouse apartment she had almost gone to bed with a perfect stranger. Both she and Clay were quite aware of that fact.

"I think we're going to work really well together," he said, interrupting her thoughts.

"As long as 'work' is the operative word," Vicki responded firmly.

Clay ignored the warning in her voice. "Why don't you let me show you around our operations," he suggested. Getting up, he left his suit jacket draped over the chair. Then he took Vicki by the elbow and escorted her out the door.

"Our office complex is right over here," he pointed to a modern glass and steel building with a long sloping roof on one side. "Since energy conservation is one of the themes of the Stone Mountain Center, we're using solar panels to power our computer facilities," he explained. "But, of course, we do have backup electricity for rainy days," he added with a chuckle.

Vicki nodded. "And DDI's contribution focuses on 'Putting Your Computer to Work.' I've been reading the series of articles that *Business Weekly* has been running for the past few weeks."

Clay shot her an amused glance. "But I bet they didn't mention that we don't quite have our act together yet. The solar air-conditioning unit we ordered isn't operating properly, and we only have enough backup electricity to cool the computer room. That's why we haven't moved in yet. But I swear, if the engineers don't have the system working by opening day, heads are going to roll."

As he pulled open the glass doors to the building, Vicki was hit with a blast of sweltering air. Suddenly she knew

why Clay had left his suit coat on the back of his chair.
Once inside she quickly began to feel beads of perspira-
tion forming on her forehead and underarms. It wouldn't
be long before her linen suit was a damp and shapeless
sack. The time for crisp formality was obviously at an
end. She unbuttoned her jacket and took it off, revealing
a scoop-necked, flowered silk blouse. Clay shot her an
appreciative glance as he steered her toward the center of
the building. Ignoring his eyes, Vicki peered with interest
at the partially set-up work areas. DDI had obviously
gone to a lot of trouble to make an impressive showing at
the center. As he opened the door to the cooler computer
room, Clay explained with the voice of a man who had
run through the same speech many times.

"We have all the latest equipment here. The most
up-to-date home and business computers are available
for the residents of our new city to use. We expect to
have a steady stream of business people and tourists who
want to see what we're doing firsthand. And Montgomery Systems is going to show them how they can stay at
home and still work at an office miles away. It's going to
be a very impressive demonstration of how computers
can really save time and energy."

Around the corner was a gallery set up with dozens of
computer arcade games.

Vicki raised a questioning eyebrow.

"There's nothing wrong with an attractive display to
get the tourists interested," he explained smoothly. "I
was able to get DDI special rates with the game manufac-
turers, and they let us preview some of their new
programs," Clay explained.

"How convenient," Vicki said dryly. "What kind of
royalty do you get on these games?"

"Oh," Clay acknowledged, "I see you've been doing
background reading on my past ventures."

"I didn't have to go out of my way. You were big as life

and the success story of the decade in the pages of *Computer Universe* last month."

"Well, don't believe everything you read," Clay admonished.

As they walked around, Vicki noticed a large sign on the far wall. It explained that all the quarters spent in the game machines would be donated to the United Nations Children's Fund. Vicki gave Clay a sidelong glance, but he said nothing. There was more to this man than all the good things that met the eye, she thought fleetingly.

Next, he showed Vicki her own office near the computer room, and she began to visualize how the Montgomery equipment would be set up. She knew her word processing system would be installed in many of the apartments throughout Stone Mountain Center. Phone lines would connect them to the main DDI computers. At these home work stations residents would be able to put in a full day's work without ever going into the office. If DDI liked the trial run, they were committed to buy a lot more Montgomery equipment for Stone Mountain Center as well as their operations across the country.

"How much do you know about Stone Mountain Center?" Clay inquired, interrupting her thoughts.

"Just what I've read."

Clay favored her with an engaging smile. "Let me take you on a short tour, then."

"Sounds like a good idea," Vicki agreed, glad for a reason to leave the sweltering building at last.

The tall, dark Southerner seemed to enjoy the chance to get away from his hectic duties for a while. As he squired her around the campuslike setting nestled in the rolling Georgia countryside, he went out of his way to be charming and courtly. Vicki found herself smiling at his jokes, despite her resolve to be on her guard. Once again, she had to admit that he was one of the handsomest men she'd ever seen.

To cool off a bit, they stopped at a small outdoor cafe in the new town's central square to sip iced tea and watch the frantic activity around them. As they sat there, three women from the DDI staff came by for a late lunch. Clay introduced them to Vicki, but she could see that all three were more interested in Clayton Harper than in his new word processing contractor.

She listened to his casual conversation, observing how he made each one of them feel she was somehow special. He's really smooth and knows it, Vicki observed to herself. Particularly, she added in warning, if there's a woman involved. She'd have to be on her toes if she didn't want to fall into his arms the way she did when they first met.

After a few moments of sipping their drinks and talking about the new town's setup, Clay leaned over, touched her slender hand, and said, "You must have been up well before the crack of dawn. And here I've been walking you for miles and talking your ear off. Would you like me to take you where you'll be staying so that you can catch a shower and a nap before dinner?"

Feeling a warm tingle where his strong hand had rested on hers, Vicki smiled gratefully. A relaxing shower sounded heavenly. "Yes, that's a great idea," she readily agreed. "I think jet lag is finally setting in."

They arose and Clay led her back into the DDI parking lot. After retrieving his coat and her briefcase from his office, he settled her down into the front seat of his silver sports car. They drove about a mile to the outskirts of the town and into a private estate set in a picturesque green valley. Clay explained that she would be staying at Magnolia House. The plantation had been built in the 1780s, and DDI had rented it to house their staff until their apartments in Stone Mountain Center could be completed.

Vicki's mind immediately shot back to her original fear that Clay had lured her out here to finish what he had started. Did he mean they would both be staying at the same house, she worried, picturing how well such an arrangement could lead to an easy seduction. But Clay seemed to read her thoughts once again.

"We've already filled up the main building with personnel who've been working on site for a few months. As much as I'd like to have you in a room next to mine, or my own room for that matter," he teased, flashing her a grin that sent warning prickles up her neck, "I'm afraid you'll be staying in an outbuilding we've been using for our newer arrivals. It's every bit as comfortable as the big house, and I think you'll like the greater privacy."

Vicki sighed with relief. That was one problem averted. Although she had no intention of getting involved with Clay Harper again, she could just imagine the extra strain on her intentions if she were staying in a room next to his. How would she be able to sleep knowing that he was so close? Did he sleep nude, she wondered irreverently as wayward images of his lean, muscular form began flashing provocatively through her mind.

I don't need any help from him; I'll seduce myself if I don't get my imagination under control, Vicki thought with annoyance. This man with his Southern charm and his dashing Rhett Butler looks was much too attractive for her own good. Just keep reminding yourself about Jerry Pratt, she warned. And don't be taken in by another pretty face. You want to return to California with a big sale for Montgomery Office Systems, but you don't intend to be part of the merchandise Clay Harper purchases, she told herself sternly.

Clay put on his directional signal and swung into a tree-lined drive. Tall pines and oaks cast a green shade on the gravel. Behind them Vicki could see and smell the delicate pink blossoms of peach trees. She looked around with anticipation. It was at least five minutes before the old house loomed into view, and then she

gave a gasp of pleasure. An enormous white Southern
mansion sat majestically on a carpet of lush green lawn.
Flanking the house were bright clusters of blooming pink
and magenta azaleas.

"It's magnificent," Vicki breathed.

"DDI likes to do things right," Clay said, pulling up to
the circular drive in front of the wide veranda. The car
purred to a stop, and he turned toward her with apprais-
ing eyes. "When we buy equipment, we buy only the
best, and we like the people who work for us to be
treated right," he drawled, his gaze in open approval
drifting over the delicate, definitely female curves of her
body.

Vicki felt her face flush. "By treating your employees
right," she retorted, "I hope you mean with dignity and
consideration."

Clay's blue eyes crinkled at the corners. "Certainly
with consideration," he allowed—without commenting
on the "dignity," she noted. Then he added in a husky
tone, "I can be very considerate, Vicki." Suddenly his
strong tanned fingers curled around her hand possessive-
ly, and before she could protest, he lifted the palm to his
lips and caressed it seductively, dropping small kisses
between her trembling fingers.

Vicki felt alarming ripples of heat penetrate her veins.
To hide her confusion, she drew her hand away from him
and snapped, "Well, if you really want to be considerate,
you'll show me to my room." Immediately she regretted
her sharp tone. It gave too much away, and she didn't
want Clay Harper to know how much his attentions
affected her.

I've got to play this cool or I'll never get through the
next three months, she warned herself. What's more, the
look of amusement on his handsome face already told
her that he had interpreted her apprehensively sensual
reaction correctly. Without another word, though, he
obligingly started up the car again and drove away from

the main house to a lane behind it that led to a long, low, white building. Although it had been recently refurbished, its irregular architecture gave away its great age.

Momentarily forgetting her unease, Vicki eyed the rectangular building and exclaimed, "This looks like it could date back over a hundred years."

"Oh, indeed it does," answered Clay, stopping the car and coming around to her side to open the door. "It was built back in the late 1700s to keep the house servants."

Vicki shot him a startled glance. "You mean I'll be staying in the old servants quarters?"

Clay took her elbow and guided her up the steps to her door. Turning to her with a teasing grin he added, "I think you'll find this room quite comfortable. The master of the house always made sure his personal servants were well taken care of."

Determinedly ignoring his innuendo, Vicki peered into the room and was pleasantly surprised. Though it was small, it was charmingly furnished with an old four-poster bed covered with a red and white handmade quilt, a pine washstand and wardrobe, and a rocker. Dark pine beams protruded from the low, whitewashed ceiling, and a colorful rag rug brightened the honey-colored planked floor. One small window was open, and an air-conditioning unit protruded out of the other. At the back of the room she could see a door leading to a small bathroom.

"It's delightful," she said approvingly. "All the charm of the Old South—but with modern convenience."

Clay nodded. "One of the smartest moves DDI made was renting this place. Otherwise we might be paying a hundred dollars plus a night to put people up in Atlanta—and in a lot less comfort. Even though it took us fifteen minutes to get here by car, we're only a twenty-minute walk to the site if you take the shortcut through the peach orchard. I'll bring in your briefcase and jacket," he added, "and introduce your neighbor if he's around."

While Clay was gone, Vicki sat down on the bed testing the mattress. "My gosh, it's real horsehair," she exclaimed. Vicki had always admired the warmth of antique American furniture, and this room suited her to a tee. It made her feel like a Southern belle, feminine and homey at the same time.

Just then her musing was interrupted by the sound of male voices. The door opened and Clay entered followed by a short, broad-shouldered man with sharp brown eyes. "This is Martin Loomis of Prentice Systems," Clay said. Vicki got up off the bed and moved toward the stranger. Automatically her hand went out to shake his thick one, but at Clay's next words she almost snatched it back.

"Prentice Systems is your competitor for the contract," he announced boldly.

Vicki blinked and her eyebrows drew together in a puzzled frown. "Competitor?"

"Yes," Clay went on nonchalantly. "DDI will be evaluating you and Martin over the next three months, and on the basis of how well you do, we'll be deciding who gets the big contract."

"And may the best man win!" Loomis chimed in with a hearty chuckle.

For the moment, Vicki could only stare at the man's self-satisfied, florid face. She felt as if she'd had the rug pulled out from under her. Ellen had said nothing about a rival bidder. Surely she would have warned her had she known. This put an entirely different complexion on the summer. It was going to be a tug-of-war. And this man looked like a truly formidable rival. The dismissing look he was casting at her told her he had no doubt about who the winner would be. Resentment seethed in Vicki's breast, and she cast Clay a scathing look. After a few more veiled pleasantries, Loomis left, and Vicki confronted Clay with hostility.

"You tricked us, didn't you?" she challenged, shooting

him a look full of angry disdain. But the imperturbable expression on Clay's face revealed no feelings of guilt.

"Surely you don't regard a little healthy competition as a trick?" he returned smoothly.

"You know very well what I mean," she countered. "You got me down here on false pretenses. My boss had no idea this was a competitive situation."

Clay's expression hardened. "If Ellen Montgomery is as sharp a business person as I think, she should be well aware that to make a sale she has to demonstrate that her product is superior. Your company is very new in the field, and I'd be foolish to accept your claims on good faith alone. Especially," he added meaningfully, "since you've shown a tendency to run out when things get too hot." His eyes drifted suggestively over the high-breasted curves of her slender torso.

To her horror Vicki found herself turning bright red under his scrutiny. In a desperate attempt to recover her dignity she said tersely, "I'll have to call Ellen and discuss the situation with her." She opened the door pointedly.

"All right, but I think you'll find your boss understands this better than you," he said, exiting.

And Clay was right. When she called Ellen a few minutes later, her reaction was relatively mild.

"I'm not surprised," she admitted. "I thought it was too good to be true. But I don't understand why he didn't make it clear in the first place. The situation would have been in black and white in most agreements of this sort, although there's technically nothing illegal about the way it was handled."

"Do you think we should pull out?" asked Vicki.

Ellen's response was vehement. "Definitely not. I have a lot of confidence in the superiority of our equipment and personnel. If the best man or woman is going to win, I'm sure it's going to be us. And I know you can do it, Vicki. Anyhow, there's a big forfeit if we throw in the towel now. We could lose our collective shirts. And as a stockholder yourself, I'd hate for you to lose everything you've worked for this past year and a half. So hang in there."

Vicki rolled her eyes, flushing hotly as she recalled how she had indeed lost her shirt—or at least the top half of her dress—that disastrous night on Clay Harper's couch. Should she tell Ellen that there was more in this than a simple business transaction? That Clay Harper's interest was more than just professional? But there seemed little point in bringing that up now. She knew that Montgomery Systems needed this contract badly, and she would do her best to see that they got it.

Even with the pressure of another competitor, Vicki felt certain she could handle the professional challenge. In fact, she was eager to show Mr. Harper just how competent she was. It was the personal aspects of this assignment that alarmed her. Could she handle those, too?

4

There were two courses of action open to her, Vicki thought wryly after she'd had a quick shower and changed into a comfortable sundress. She could spend the rest of the afternoon and the evening worrying about how she was going to cope, or she could start acclimating herself to the situation. The latter seemed a much more positive approach. Maybe things would look a little brighter after a good dinner.

It might have been the power of suggestion, or maybe it was her scant airplane lunch hours ago, for Vicki suddenly felt her stomach rumble. Glancing at her watch, she was surprised to find that it was almost seven forty-five. She'd forgotten about the time difference.

Taking only a few moments to reapply her makeup and brush her auburn hair, Vicki gathered up her purse and headed toward the main building. What if Clay were there, she wondered. She'd have to come up with some casual way of letting him know that she'd talked to Ellen and now understood the score. But she'd be damned if

she'd give him an opportunity to say, "I told you so."
Furthermore, she'd have to be extra careful not to give
him the impression that there would be anything but
business between them.

Vicki was still trying out various ways of accomplishing
all that when she reached the lobby of Magnolia House.
Stopping to consult the restaurant schedule posted in a
glass case to one side of the large foyer, she discovered
that she only had a few minutes to spare before the last
dinner sitting.

Lucky I got here in time, she congratulated herself as
she followed the signs to the Garden Room. It turned out
to be a long lattice-and-glass-enclosed porch set with
white linen-covered tables and decorated with hanging
pots of gracefully trailing ferns.

Stopping at the doorway, Vicki scanned the room.
Apparently most of the Stone Mountain staff opted for
the earlier sittings. The elegant dining room was no more
than a third filled. To her relief, the few present didn't
include the maddening Clay Harper.

One table of young men and women noticed her
hesitancy at the door and motioned for her to join them.
With a grateful smile, Vicki accepted their invitation. It'd
be so much nicer to have dinner with a group than eating
alone, and they'd be an insurance policy as well. If Clay
made a late entrance, she wouldn't have to handle him
by herself. He'd probably be on his best behavior around
his employees, careful not to let on how he planned to
use his business influence to gain private advantage with
her.

The thought made her expression sour.

"Why so serious?" a sandy-haired young man with
wire-framed glasses inquired as he pulled out the seat
next to his. "I'm Ted," he continued, not really seeming
to expect an answer, "and this motley crew is Jan,
Evelyn, Phil, and Courtney. We're all slaves in DDI's
programming department."

Vicki acknowledged the introductions with a smile as she sat down.

"What brings you to Stone Mountain Center?" the attractive brunette named Evelyn asked with friendly interest. "Are you going to join our team?"

"I'm with Montgomery Systems," Vicki began, but the rest of her planned explanation was lost in a flurry of comments.

"So you're competing with that creep Martin Loomis for the word processing contract," Ted said.

Vicki's eyebrows shot together. The frank comment caught her by surprise.

"Everybody's been talking about it for days," Evelyn interjected, noticing her expression. "With his overbearing attitude, Loomis hasn't been winning any popularity contests around here."

"Glad to know we've got someone else to root for," she told Vicki with a conspiratorial smile.

The chatter was interrupted by the arrival of the waiter, who asked for their main dish selections. Tonight, he informed them in a thick Southern accent, their choices were chicken and dumplings, barbecued pork, and fried flounder. For the newcomer's benefit, Ted explained that the rest of the meal would be served family style.

Vicki was glad that the center of attention had momentarily shifted from herself to the waiter. So everybody down here knew about the word processing competition, she told herself. That wasn't going to make her job any easier. And she could imagine how seriously Martin Loomis was taking this whole affair. She'd seen his type before. Success was everything, and a public failure would be a double defeat. He'd be even more formidable as an opponent than she'd imagined. Clay Harper had really put her in an awkward position. Why had he done this to her?

As if reading her troubled thoughts, Evelyn turned to Vicki after the orders had been taken. "Everybody was really surprised when this turned out to be a competitive bid," the young woman confided.

Vicki inclined her head questioningly.

"Yeah," Ted seconded. "Loomis thought he had it all sewed up. But that was before Clay Harper came on board. He'd evidently been really impressed with your demonstration out in L.A. and insisted that Montgomery be given a shot at the contract. I understand he put his vice-presidency on the line to get you down here."

Vicki's eyes widened. "Surely you're kidding?"

Ted shook his head. "No. One thing you'll find out about the staff at Magnolia House is that we have a grapevine that would put Sing Sing to shame. Everybody knows what everybody else is doing—even before they're doing it."

The group at the table chuckled appreciatively. But the revelation gave Vicki a lot to ponder. She knew she wasn't much of a conversationalist during the rest of dinner. She was still deep in thought after the programmers had finished dessert and coffee.

"Want to join us for a walk around the grounds?" Ted invited as everyone stood up.

"I think I should take a rain check," Vicki demurred. "It's been a long day, and I still have a lot of unpacking to do."

Her new acquaintances shook their heads sympathetically. "You're right," Ted agreed. "You probably need to get settled in. Maybe some other time."

Vicki made her escape with mixed feelings. The information on Clay Harper's behind-the-scenes string pulling had taken her by surprise. As she hung up blouses and folded lingerie into drawers, images of her rakish-looking new boss came unbidden to her mind.

What were Clay's real motives in getting her down here? He had gone to a great deal of trouble—more than she would have believed—to give her company an opportunity to compete. Either he was extremely impressed with Montgomery's new system, or he was waging a hell of a campaign to get her into bed. Could that really be it, she asked herself, looking down to see that she had crumpled her new lace slip into a ball. Smoothing it out again, she tried to smooth her own twisted thoughts.

After all, she reasoned, if Clay only had seduction in mind, he was laying a quarter of a million dollars of someone else's money on the line. That was quite a price tag for one female computer analyst—in or out of bed. The thought was reassuring. He couldn't have brought her all the way across the country just for that.

But motives could be complicated, she told herself, her mind flashing back suddenly to the passionate scene in his hotel room in L.A. He had wanted her then. And if she were honest, she would admit that she had wanted him, too. She had tried to convince herself that it wasn't true, and when she'd been so busy in Santa Barbara getting ready for this contract, she had almost succeeded. After all, there had been no time for anything else but work. But it had only taken five minutes in Clayton Harper's presence to remind her how susceptible she was to his brand of Southern persuasion.

With a shiver, she remembered the way he'd dropped little kisses on her fingers when they'd pulled up at Magnolia House. She had reacted to him as if the weeks of separation had never existed. And he must have known it. Obviously she was going to get no help from him in keeping this relationship on a strictly business level. That was going to be her responsibility. Knowing her overpowering reaction to the man, it wasn't going to be easy, but it would just have to be that way.

The questions were still churning in her mind when she finally climbed into bed.

The shrill ring of the telephone on the night stand brought Vicki abruptly back to consciousness. With a start she looked at the digital clock across the room and groaned. It was already almost nine.

Getting up early had never been a problem for her. Unfortunately, she'd forgotten about the time difference. Evidently her body was still working on Pacific time. "Yes?" she managed, trying to sound as businesslike as possible under the circumstances. But apparently she couldn't fool Barry. "Your turn to be caught sleeping," he teased.

"Okay, you've got me," she admitted, with an exaggerated sigh. "Anything important happening?"

"Only that C. L. Harper dropped by to see how we were doing. I covered for you and told him you'd stepped out of the office for a minute. But you'd better do the pep step now. He's stopping back at ten o'clock with the director of public relations."

Even while he spoke, Vicki was throwing back the covers and swinging her shapely legs over the edge of the high bed.

"Thanks, Barry" she acknowledged. "I owe you one. I'll get there before Harper does."

What should she wear, Vicki debated as she let the warm needles of shower spray wake her up. On one hand, she wanted to look professional when Clay Harper brought his PR person by. But she knew that a nice suit wouldn't stand up to a day of installing computer equipment. She'd be better off in slacks, she finally decided, after toweling herself dry and thumbing through her wardrobe. Then she looked at her watch again. She really didn't have time to dally. Her good pair of jeans and a soft plaid shirt would just have to do.

Vicki was glad she'd listened to Clay Harper's description of the shortcut between Magnolia House and the Stone Mountain Center. However, once she reached the path through the orchards, she was sorry she had to hurry. Stone Mountain stood magnificently in front of her, dwarfing everything in sight. The air was filled with the delicate fragrance of newly blossoming peach trees, and the pinkish blossoms against a cloudless blue sky were a feast for her eyes. It was the kind of thing one missed in Southern California, where spring was less of an event because it was just a continuation of habitually mild weather.

As she pushed open the door that connected her office to the main corridor of the DDI complex, she noticed that the air conditioning was working. Well, at least that was one stroke of luck.

Another pleasant surprise was waiting at her desk—a cup of coffee and a cream cheese danish. Barry had come to her rescue again. Looking through the glass partition that gave her a good view of the computer room, she spotted her technician.

"Thanks!" she told him, pushing open the door that gave direct access to the operations area. "Looks like I owe you another one."

"I expect you to remember that if we hit a snag in the installation," the wiry young man returned.

"Now wait a minute," Vicki began. But he had already turned back to direct his crew in uncrating cartons of Montgomery equipment.

As she settled into the swivel chair at her desk and picked up the coffee, Vicki surveyed her surroundings. Right now the Montgomery corner of the computer facility looked like the loading dock of an extremely disorganized warehouse. Close to forty crates of equipment in various stages of being unpacked littered the area. But she knew that by the end of the day Barry would have turned the chaos into neatly assembled word processing units ready for installation around the Stone Mountain center.

Her view of the main computer room was almost

blocked. But between the crates she caught glimpses of the DDI operations staff loading magnetic tapes, carrying listings to the service window, and running the main computer console. The whole system looked unusually efficient, and she caught herself craning her neck for a better view before she realized she was wasting valuable time. Get to work, she told herself sternly. You'll be able to get acquainted with the DDI setup after your own system is operational.

Just then Barry tapped on the glass partition separating her executive office from the machine room. "Do you want me to put one whole unit together before I finish unpacking the rest?" he questioned.

Vicki nodded. "Yes," she began. But Barry shook his head and pointed to his ear. Vicki raised her voice several decibels so that she could be heard through the glass partition. "Yes," she began again. "Then I can test out that new diagnostic package the development staff handed me on the way out the door."

The technician went back to work, and Vicki dug into her briefcase for the computer listing she needed to run the test. She was three pages deep into the documentation when she felt a familiar tingle on the back of her neck. She spun her high-backed padded chair around to face the door behind her and lifted her eyes to encounter Clay Harper's sky blue gaze. His look held her captive for a long moment, and it was several seconds before she realized that he was not alone. Standing in the corridor behind him was a beautiful young woman wearing a wheat-colored suit and a navy print blouse. Her shoulder-length blond hair was softly curled, providing a golden frame for her oval face. Vicki noticed that the willowy blonde stood only a few inches shorter than the young executive. Clay ambled into the room, followed by his briskly stepping companion.

"Vicki, I'd like you to meet our PR director, Gail

Patterson. Gail, this is Vicki Johnson from Montgomery Systems," he said, performing the necessary introductions.

Suddenly Vicki was sorry she had decided on her casual outfit. Both Gail's image and her manner told Vicki that the other woman was ready for business, and that made her own jeans and shirt seem decidedly out of place.

Gail must have noticed Vicki's expression. However, like Clay, she had the Southern charm to put even a new acquaintance at ease immediately. "You look like you're in for a day of hard work," she observed, in a soft Georgia accent, making the statement sound like a compliment.

Vicki couldn't help responding with a relieved grin. "A skirt just won't do when you have to crawl around under the terminals checking the connections," she agreed.

"So how do you like it here so far?" Gail asked, casting a look around the Montgomery office.

"I don't know about the working conditions yet," Vicki answered honestly, giving Clay a pointed look. "But the food at Magnolia House is wonderful. I'll be lucky if I don't gain ten pounds while I'm here."

"My, isn't it the truth," Gail agreed. "Southern cooking is the best in the world, but then I'm a little biased."

"You've got a reason to be biased," Clay interjected. "You could turn scrawny old stewing chicken into squab under glass."

Vicki looked from Clay to Gail, puzzled at his display of familiarity. Was he trying to tell her something about their relationship? Or was it just second nature for him to come on with every woman he met? Gail looked like the type who could have almost any man she wanted. Did she want Clay?

But Gail's next words confused her even more. "Now, Clay," she admonished playfully, "you're going to give

your new contractor a false impression. She'll think I'm a
regular cordon bleu chef rather than the hominy and grits
cook that I really am." Then she turned back to Vicki.
"I'm late for a press conference, but I did want to stop by
and meet you. Now, if there's anything you need, or if
you just want to chat, give me a call. Here's my number."
Pulling an antique silver case from her purse, she extracted a pale gray card and handed it to Vicki.

"See y'all later," she called over her shoulder on her
way out the door.

When the young woman had left, Clay pulled up a
straight back chair and sat down disturbingly close to
Vicki's desk.

"Gail has been in on this project almost from the
beginning. She really knows her way around. She can be
a tremendous help to a newcomer. I know she was to
me," he commented with a perfectly straight face and a
twinkle in his eye.

I'll bet, Vicki thought, as she nodded noncommittally.

"But as much as Gail knows, she still doesn't have my
unique perspective on how I'd like this test project set
up."

"I assume you're going to share that with me?" Vicki
questioned, working hard to keep a hostile edge out of
her voice. She couldn't banish her suspicions of the
man's motives. And it didn't help that despite herself, she
found her eyes eating up his dark good looks like a
starving person.

"By all means. How about over dinner tonight?" Clay
invited, leaning forward slightly in his chair.

Vicki was about to respond with a defensive refusal
when she had second thoughts. Here was the perfect
opportunity to set up her own ground rules with Clay
Harper. Maybe if she let him know right at the beginning
that there would be no continuation of their torrid little
scene in L.A., he'd abandon his pursuit.

"I'm looking forward to it," Vicki said with conviction.

There was so much work to do that she had time for only a quick sandwich at her desk. And as the afternoon wore on, she was indeed glad that she'd decided on the jeans. The prototype system had apparently been wired incorrectly, and Barry insisted that she crouch behind the partially assembled unit and hold various circuit boards in place while he resoldered the connections.

After twenty minutes of that uncomfortable position, Vicki decided anything was preferable. So when one of the other technicians came back to report problems with a printer, she seized the excuse to move on to other less physical activities. At first the machine in question seemed to be printing in invisible ink. When she removed the cartridge, however, she found out where all the ink had gone—onto her hands.

Wonderful! she thought. Clay Harper is going to assume his date spent the afternoon in a coal mine instead of a computer room. The observation made her check her watch. Heavens, it was already past five o'clock, and Clay had told her to be ready by six since they'd be driving into Atlanta. She'd better get a move on.

"I think we can call it quits for today," she informed her crew as she tried to remove the excess ink from her hands on the large textured tissue designed for wiping off computer equipment.

Her announcement was greeted with sighs of relief from her hard-working staff. The first day of setting up equipment was never much fun, but today had been particularly trying for everybody.

With only fifteen minutes to spare before Clay's arrival, Vicki stepped out of the shower. The stimulating water massage had done wonders to revive her aching body. And luckily she'd brought a small scrub brush that had removed all traces of ink from her hands, even if it had almost taken off a layer of skin in the process. But she'd have to hurry now, or Clay would find her in her underwear.

She used up half of her precious time applying make-up. The effect was well worth it though, she decided, stepping back from the mirror to assess her wide-set emerald eyes now accented by deep sable mascara, cinnamon-tinted lips, and thick auburn hair that had been carefully coaxed into an artless cascade. She had created such a polished look that no one could doubt her self-confidence. If she was going to get her relationship with Clay onto the right track, she'd need all the self-confidence she could muster. Unfortunately, while she was running late, Clay was five minutes early. His knock on the door did indeed catch her in her satin slip.

"Just a moment," she called out in a panic, reaching into her closet for the lime green, silky knit dress she'd decided to wear. In her haste to get presentable, she pulled up the zipper too fast and it caught on the delicate fabric in the small of her back where she could barely reach. Given enough time, she probably could have worked it down. But time was what she didn't have. That point was brought sharply home by Clay's second impatient knock.

Vicki stifled the urge to yank at the zipper. That would just ruin the dress. The only solution was to ask Clay's help. After stepping into her strappy white sling backs, Vicki tentatively opened the door. But when she saw Clay Harper clad in a well-fitting charcoal gray suit with a pale blue dress shirt leaning indolently in her doorway, a faint blush spread across her cheeks.

"You look terrific," he drawled giving her a close inspection that made her vividly aware of her state of partial undress.

The flush across her high cheekbones deepened.

"Only from the front," she confessed with embarrassment. "I'm afraid I need your help again."

"Oh?" he questioned, stepping into the room and closing the door behind him.

"Before you get the wrong idea," Vicki interposed, "I only need help with my zipper. It's stuck."

Clay gave her a speculative glance. "Haven't we played this scene before? I seem to remember acting lady's maid in L.A.," he reminded, "a task I performed quite well if memory serves me right."

"This time your performance appraisal will depend on speed," Vicki countered, unable to keep the edge of annoyance out of her voice.

Noting her reaction to the situation, Clay became very businesslike. "Turn around," he ordered.

Vicki obeyed. She could feel his fingers working carefully at the zipper, trying to free it from the soft material without making a pull in the fabric.

She tried to focus her attention on the American primitive painting across the room, but she was powerfully aware of Clay's body directly behind her and the brush of his fingers as they inadvertently touched the smooth skin of her back. Keeping her body from quivering every time he touched her was getting to be almost impossible. And Vicki found herself clenching her hands as she concentrated on not reacting to Clay Harper in the way her body wanted so much to react.

She would like to have urged him to hurry. But she didn't trust her voice. All she could do was stand there like a statue, waiting for him to finish.

One of his hands moved to her hair, gently pushing it over her shoulder. "I've almost got it," he whispered, his breath warm against her neck. "But I don't want to catch this gorgeous mane of yours."

"Clay, please . . ." Vicki began.

But at that moment the zipper came free of the

entangling fabric and Clay drew it smoothly up to the clasp. Vicki took a step forward to increase the distance between the two of them, but Clay put a restraining hand on her shoulder.

"Let me get the hook and eye," he murmured.

"Thanks for your help, but I believe I can do the rest of it myself," Vicki insisted, reaching to the back of her dress and completing the operation.

She turned and picked up her purse, indicating that she was ready to leave. Taking his cue, Clay opened the door and escorted her out to his waiting car. The mere act of leaving the confinement of her room seemed to dissipate a bit of the tension between them. And to her surprise, as they drove toward Atlanta, Vicki found that as long as she kept the conversation steered to work-related topics, things were fine.

The restaurant Clay had chosen was high atop a newly completed office building on Peachtree Street. The Lion's Lair was lavishly appointed with a marble entrance fountain flowing into a crystal pool which diners had to cross on a little footbridge. The dining room itself was divided into many intimate alcoves fitted out with small octagonal tables and comfortable leather armchairs.

As they followed the maître d' to their seats, Clay leaned over and whispered to Vicki, "It's not just empty ambiance. The food's excellent, too."

Vicki soon discovered that Clay hadn't exaggerated. The pâté maison, steak Diane, and asparagus hollandaise she ordered were beyond compare and the Cabernet Sauvignon Clay selected was the perfect accompaniment to their meal. Vicki found herself enjoying both the food and Clay's company very much, and that thought brought her up short. The only reason she had agreed to come, she reminded herself sternly, was to make sure that C. L. Harper understood the ground rules for their working relationship. Taking a sip of wine for courage,

Vicki brought up the all-important topic she had been planning to introduce.

"You know I really was upset by the way you got me down here," she began.

Clay raised a questioning eyebrow. "Oh?"

The noncommittal response told her he wasn't going to be much help.

"I think you should have let me know that you were managing this project before I was committed to coming," she tried again.

Clay leaned back in his leather chair and gave her a measured look. "Would you have come if you'd known?" he asked pointedly.

Maybe not, she admitted to herself taking another sip of the red wine, but she was damned if she'd admit that to Clayton Harper.

"Don't you think that things run more smoothly when everybody knows what to expect?" she met his question with one of her own.

"There's more to this than just the omission of my name from the contract," Clay persisted, trying to read the emotion-filled expression in her green eyes.

He was giving her the opportunity to say what she really meant, Vicki realized. Did she have the courage to tell him? Before she could lose her nerve, she plunged ahead.

"All right," she conceded. "Back in L.A. you asked me why I was so sensitive about your comment on beauty and brains. Do you remember?"

He nodded, his eyes still intent on her face. The close scrutiny made her task even harder. She reached for her water glass to moisten her suddenly dry throat before continuing. "Well, my negative reaction wasn't just to what you said that evening." Vicki chose her next words carefully. "I have real cause to be concerned where male employers are involved."

"That's a pretty sweeping statement," he said, challenging her generalization.

"Well," Vicki continued, "in my first job after college my boss tried to make 'bed partner' part of my job description. And when I turned down his wonderful offer he made life hell for me. Unfortunately, I was in a position where I couldn't just quit. My brother-in-law had paid for my college education, and he needed the money because his own business was just getting off the ground."

Clay's blue eyes darkened. "That sounds like a rotten deal all right. But you know, Vicki, you can't judge every business situation in terms of one bad experience."

"I'm not," she found herself defending her position. "But can you honestly say that your method of getting me down here was calculated to inspire confidence on my part?"

Her accusation came closer to home than Clay would have liked. A frown wrinkled his forehead.

"From your point of view, I guess it does look awfully suspicious," he conceded. "Actually, I did want to see you again. But in addition to that, I honestly wanted to give Montgomery a chance at this contract."

Clay hesitated for a moment, and Vicki could see a smile quirking the corners of his lips.

"What are you thinking?" she asked.

"I'm thinking that even an intelligent, highly successful, creative genius like me occasionally makes mistakes."

Vicki couldn't help grinning back. She had been prepared to do battle with the new vice-president at DDI, but Clay's ready admission had defused her ammunition. There were few men who would have had the guts to laugh at themselves with such an outrageous statement. Vicki studied Clay's ruggedly masculine features with new respect. Where do we go from here, she asked herself.

Their minds seemed to be on the same track because Clay answered her unspoken question. "On the one hand, you've made me realize that I've put you in an unfair position," he began. "But then again, I do want to get better acquainted. I hope you don't hold that against me."

Vicki shook her head. What could she say after all? If she were honest, she would admit that she wanted to get to know him better, too.

"Why don't we start off with a clean slate?" he suggested. "It'll be strictly business on the job, I promise. But that doesn't mean that we can't get to know each other on our own time. What about it?"

Vicki found herself hesitating. Clay was the most attractive man she'd met in a long time, and on one level she was eager to continue the relationship. But could there really be no strings attached?

"What assurances do I have?" she finally asked.

"Just the word of a Southern gentleman," Clay drawled.

"Are you really a *gentleman?*" Vicki asked.

"Well you'll just have to find out, won't you," he proposed wickedly.

Vicki smiled. "We can give it a try, but you'd better be on your best behavior."

"Only at the office, my dear." He grinned broadly.

Vicki blushed and changed the subject. "Well, I guess I'm not really sorry you brought me out here. This is really an exciting place to be."

"It is, isn't it," Clay agreed, his face lighting up with enthusiasm. "It's like being on the edge of the future. Imagine what a big change this concept will make in everyone's daily lives." His hands gestured expressively. "Just think, disabled people who can't get around can earn their living with dignity in their own surroundings and"—his eyes glowed with inner conviction—"mothers who need to earn a living will be able to stay with their small children and work at home. Families can spend their day together—and that's something I feel very strongly about."

Vicki listened raptly to the visions that he described with almost boyish enthusiasm. Leaning her elbow on the table, she propped her chin on the upturned palm of her hand. She was seeing a whole new side of Clay—a side she found infinitely attractive. He really was committed to helping people, and Stone Mountain was a symbol of that dedication.

Time seemed to fly by, and before Vicki knew it the waiter was handing Clay the check and wishing them a pleasant evening.

As Clay helped Vicki back into his car, his fingers lingered for a moment longer than necessary on the silky material of her sleeve. Once inside the darkly intimate interior of the powerful sedan, he wanted nothing more than to turn and take her in his arms. But he forced himself to keep his hands firmly on the steering wheel.

Careful, don't scare her off again, he warned himself. Victoria Johnson's not like the other women you've taken to bed. She's something very special, but she's also had a very bad experience. Go too fast and you'll get nowhere with her.

"So how did you get into the computer field?" Vicki asked, interrupting his train of thought. The silence before he answered was so long that she thought perhaps he hadn't heard her question.

"I must have inherited my interest in electronics from my father," Clay finally answered, shifting into high gear as they pulled onto the expressway leading out from downtown Atlanta. "And I probably got my drive from him as well," he added, unable to keep the irony he felt out of his voice.

Vicki picked up on the note of discord. "What's wrong with that?" she wanted to know.

"There's too much of the old man in me," Clay shot back, surprising Vicki with the vehemence of his reply.

There must be something about his relationship with his father that he hadn't come to terms with, she reasoned, shifting uneasily in her plush bucket seat.

"Sorry," he apologized. "But you hit on one of my sore subjects. Few people realize what it's like to be the only son of a dynamo father. Everybody was always measuring me against his successes. That's one reason I refused to take over his empire. I wanted to make a mark for myself in a new field."

"Well, you've certainly done that," Vicki conceded, thinking that she understood this enigmatic man a little better. But she still only had part of the picture. And she realized that Clay Harper was not about to fill in all the details.

Most of the lights were off at Magnolia House by the time they pulled into the small parking area behind the low annex building where Vicki's room was located. At the beginning of the ride home, Clay had vowed that he would not rush things between the two of them. But the personal nature of the conversation about his father had weakened his self-control. When Vicki turned and put her hand on his arm, he was all too aware of the desirable woman sitting next to him.

"I want to thank you for dinner," she began innocently.

"That can easily be arranged," Clay found himself saying.

Before she could move back, he pulled her into his arms and covered her soft lips with his demanding ones. Vicki opened her mouth to protest. But that only provided convenient entry for his questing tongue. The erotic power of the kiss seemed to heighten all of Vicki's senses. Suddenly she was vividly aware of the brush of his mustache against her upper lip, the spicy smell of his aftershave lotion, and the sound of her own blood pounding in her ears. It was as though she were enveloped in a warm cocoon created by Clay Harper. And it was so very tempting to remain there with him. He had awakened her feelings in a way no man had been able to in a long time. And her body longed to silence the questions that her mind kept raising. Yet the rational part of her would not be entirely restrained. Part of her protested that she mustn't let this happen—not yet.

Clay's lips left hers to trace the line of her jaw and nibble seductively at the lobe of her ear. "You smell of wildflowers and honey," he whispered, his breath warm against her hair.

With every ounce of willpower, she tried to ignore the havoc he was creating.

"I thought we agreed—" she began.

But he cut off her half-formed thought with a low chuckle, as his fingers buried themselves in her long auburn tresses. "We're not on company time now," he pointed out, with a logic that her body found appealing.

"Clay, please," Vicki tried again. She felt as though she were hanging on to a ledge by her fingernails, and the drop below was frightening. Clay Harper had the power to push her over the edge. She knew that. Her only chance was to persuade him to stop.

But he seemed intent on ignoring her protests. With slow sensuality his warm tongue traced the whorls of her ear, sending little darts of intense pleasure through her being. Then his lips moved lower, blazing a path of fire down her neck to linger on the pulse point he found at its base. At the same time she could feel his hands on her back through the silky material of her dress as though there was nothing between them. She remembered the feel of his hands on her breasts, and part of her ached for him to repeat that intimate caress.

As if reading her mind, his fingers began to move tantalizingly up and down her ribs, each time coming closer and closer to her breasts but not actually touching them. The teasing was as effective as anything he could have done. Vicki felt her nipples harden in an anticipatory response, and she was unable to prevent a moan of protest from escaping her lips.

Clay knew what she wanted. His fingers began to caress the underside of her swelling curves, moving upward now until he could feel her hardened nipples through the sheer fabric of her dress.

"My God, Vicki, I can't help myself," he groaned. As one hand continued the erotic attention to her breasts, the other began an exploration of her leg, inching upward toward the knot of fire he had ignited in the very core of her femininity. Vicki's breath quickened in growing sexual excitement. Unconsciously moving closer to his hypnotizing touch, she felt the gear stick dig uncomfortably into her thigh, and the stab of pain brought her back to reality. Was she really sitting in a darkened parking lot letting Clay Harper practically make love to her? She had set out this evening to try and make Clay understand why something like this was impossible, and look where she had ended up. The man had disarmed her with his honesty and humor, but that was no excuse. What kind of trouble was she asking for?

Pulling away from Clay, she rubbed the sore spot on her thigh.

"Are you all right?" he asked, reaching over to massage gently the bruised skin. She could hear the concern in his voice, but also the husky passion.

"No, I'm not all right," she snapped, removing his hand from her thigh and pulling her skirt back down over her knees. Without stopping for a reply, she pulled open the door.

"Wait," Clay urged.

But she was not about to give him a second chance to seduce her. With as much dignity as possible she swung her legs out of the car, rose to her feet, and closed the door firmly behind her.

5

~~~~~~~~~~~~~~

The following morning, after a night of tossing and turning, Vicki got up at the first gray light of dawn and sought the haven of her office. She breathed a sigh of relief when she pulled away from Magnolia House without encountering any of its other residents—especially Clay. After last night's debacle, he was the last person she wanted to see.

The fear of meeting him was still in her mind as she neared his new office in the empty corridor of the DDI building. Vicki noticed that a bronze nameplate on the door already marked it as C. L. Harper's private domain. She held her breath as she walked by. Mercifully, all she heard was her own echoing footsteps. The handsome Southerner was apparently not the type of executive who rose with the birds. Or at least, she amended as she recalled his early visit of the day before, he wasn't this morning.

Once in the safety of her own quarters, she threw

herself into work. To quiet her jumbled emotions, she tackled a pile of filing she'd left for the administrative assistant she had on loan from DDI. While the coffee brewed, her busy hands created order, even though her emotions lay scattered in chaos.

It was impossible to banish the memory of Clay's fiery kisses. Her cheeks reddened as she remembered the feel of his exploring hands. Despite her efforts to banish the recollection of his sensual touch, though, she couldn't file it away in a dark corner of her mind in the same efficient manner she was relegating the papers that cluttered her desk to a dark cabinet. At least she could be thankful she had the office to herself. Barry was scouring Atlanta's electronic outlets for a specialized interface chip needed to hook up their system to DDI's network.

Only when the office was straightened and she'd downed two cups of black coffee could Vicki concentrate on her tasks for the day. Work had always been her salvation. In college, whenever she'd been troubled, she'd cloistered herself with her studies. As often as not the problem currently troubling her had simply gone away. Plunging into her job was the solution she automatically turned to now. Pulling out design plans, she began to pour over them, scribbling in changes and taking notes on possible improvements.

Three hours later, deep in thought over a possible problem in the configuration, she was jarred from her reverie by a heavy rap on the office door. Her heart seemed to leap into her throat as her head jerked up and she eyed the closed barrier. Who was on the other side of it? Was it Clay? Suddenly she was disgusted with herself. Why was she letting the man make such a nervous wreck of her? She wasn't a naive teenager, she was a grown woman, for God's sake—all grown up and perfectly capable of handling the situation.

Pulling herself up sharp, she combed her fingers

through her thick auburn hair, straightened her collar, and called out in a cool voice, "Come in."

But when the door was pushed open, it was not the tall, commanding figure of C. L. Harper but the broad, bulky form of Martin Loomis that stood revealed.

"You're quite the early bird," he remarked, giving her a practiced smile. "I thought I saw you slip out at the crack of dawn this morning, but I was still bleary-eyed and half asleep."

The knowledge that he'd seen her gave Vicki an unpleasant start. Her heart began to thud. Could he have observed what went on in Clay's car last night? The last thing she needed now was to be compromised professionally by Clay's attentions. As always, she overreacted to that kind of embarrassment, and she felt her hands go cold. Staring up into her business rival's shuttered eyes, she looked for some clue to his real thoughts—a leer or a look of knowing male amusement. But his round face gave nothing away. Taking a deep, calming breath, she pulled herself together and replied evenly to his question.

"I had some work to do and thought I'd get an early start."

"I can see you're going to be a formidable competitor," he remarked casually as he strolled further into the room. "I'm going to have to adopt an early to bed, early to rise schedule to keep up with you." He moved in back of her and peered over her shoulder at the design she'd been working on. "That's a rather unusual layout with the executive work station," he commented with surprise. "We have something very similar in our setup. Does your configuration have large capacity storage as well as floppy discs?" he questioned, trying to read the fine print on her layout.

He gave her a knowing look and moved over to the work table where she had stacked some other plans. Unrolling one, he began to scrutinize it with narrowed eyes. Vicki watched uneasily as he combed thick fingers through his sparse blond hair. She didn't like him nosing around the office. What's more, that particular plan was both innovative and central to Montgomery's project at Stone Mountain.

With a decisive movement, she pushed back her chair and rose to her feet. Seconds later, she had taken the plans from Loomis's thick hands and rolled them firmly back into a tight scroll.

"Proprietary information," she murmured with a dry smile. "I don't like giving away mine, and I suspect you don't like giving away yours," she added, inserting the rolled sheet into a cardboard cylinder and tapping it in firmly.

Loomis's face lit up with a surprisingly appealing, boyish grin. The man's not a salesman for nothing, thought Vicki, and that conclusion was affirmed by his next words.

"Just because we're business rivals doesn't mean we can't be friendly," he proposed. "After all, we have a lot in common," he gestured expansively at the plans and manuals strewn around the room. "I have to shuffle the same kind of paper you do, and I'm under the same kinds of pressure you are. This contract is important to my company, too," he said, raising his hands palm upward. "What's more, my promotion depends on it. I'm kind of an old warhorse at this game." He gave a deprecating laugh. "I'm forty-seven and I'm not getting any younger. Unlike you, I haven't got most of my career in front of me, so it's now or never," he added, leaning against the file cabinet and looking down at his feet.

Vicki studied him warily. Was the man trying to play on her sympathy? Was this a new ploy or was he sincere? Despite his soulful look, something told her not to trust him.

"Well, I can appreciate what you're going through.

Even though I'm younger than you, I know about pressure. But that doesn't mean—"

Before she could finish her disclaimer, Martin reached out and squeezed her hand like a reassuring older brother. "Why don't we rise above it?" he offered. "How about letting me take you out to lunch so we can talk about our mutual headaches? We're going to be seeing a lot of each other in the next few weeks so why don't we do our best to make this a pleasant association?"

Vicki turned his request over in her mind quickly. Why not? she asked herself. There was no point in making an enemy of this man by refusing. An hour in his company at lunch might save her some future aggravation. "Okay," she agreed politely, "but I have a few more details to clear up here before I can get away."

Loomis nodded affably. "Fine, fine with me. I'll stop by for you in an hour. Do you like Oriental cuisine? There's a little place not far from here that has the best Szechuan this side of Chinatown."

"Great," Vicki agreed. "See you in an hour," she added as he turned to leave. But when he'd disappeared into the hallway and she'd closed the door behind him, she immediately picked up the phone and dialed Ellen's office.

As soon as she heard Ellen's warm hello, Vicki felt reassured. Even though Ellen was three thousand miles away, the older woman was available to give advice when it was needed. And now was such a time. Quickly, Vicki described Loomis's visit to her office. "I'm really suspicious of the man, Ellen. Could you do some checking up on him so I have some idea of what I'm dealing with? I don't quite trust him."

"Sure thing," her boss agreed. "I'll have Hank make a few calls this morning. Seems to me he's mentioned some stories about the guy, but I don't remember what. I'll get back to you as soon as I can."

There was a pause and Vicki could picture the tall stately woman leaning back in her chair and scribbling a note on the engraved pad of paper she always kept on her desk.

"I know this is tough on you, Vicki, but you're doing a good job, so hang in there," Ellen said as she hung up.

Vicki smiled. She knew that Ellen had been a cheerleader in college, and when the occasion warranted it still showed. She had a way of offering the kind of encouragement that made her employees want to go the distance for her.

That was the mood Vicki was in when Martin Loomis returned. But as her portly rival took her elbow to steer her through the outer door of DDI, the twosome almost bumped into the rapidly striding figure of Clayton Harper.

"Sorry about that," Clay apologized, his blue eyes sweeping over the couple and lingering on the hand Martin had placed on Vicki's arm. "I was rushing to get in because I overslept." His gaze shifted accusingly to Vicki's face. "It took me a long time to get to sleep last night," he added after a significant pause. Vicki felt her cheeks get hot. She'd had some trouble getting to sleep herself.

"Well, you're the boss," Martin replied jovially. "You're allowed to make your own hours. But if you've missed breakfast, you're welcome to join us for lunch. We're on our way to The Jade Gate."

Clay rocked back on his heels and glanced at Vicki's embarrassed expression. Then a slow smile spread across his chiseled features. "That sounds like a great idea. I could use some solid food. Get a table for four and I'll meet you there in a few minutes. I'll bring Gail."

A pang of jealousy shot through Vicki that she immediately tried to squelch. She liked Gail, but that didn't make the sleek blonde's seemingly close relationship with Clay any easier to accept.

Wait a minute, she brought herself up short, here I go again letting Clay upset me. He's not my lover and he isn't going to be. She stiffened her spine defiantly. So I'm not going to be so stupid as to let myself be jealous of Gail. In fact, if Gail is really serious about Clay, perhaps I should warn her that he's admitted he's not the marrying type and that when he's not with her he's been making passes at me.

She was still mulling this problem over as they entered the restaurant and followed the maître d' to an intimate booth. She and Martin ordered drinks and were just beginning to sip them as Clay walked in with Gail Patterson on his arm.

As before, Gail looked stunning, dressed in a crisp white linen suit with a red blouse that accentuated her willowy curves. Despite her resolve not to be envious of Gail, Vicki felt her heart sink. Next to this Southern beauty she felt dowdy—an image that had been totally foreign to her. Never in the past had she had ever felt unequal to another woman, nor had she ever wasted time measuring her looks against another female's. That she was doing so now was a powerful demonstration of just how much Clay was affecting her. The fact of her vulnerability made her react with resentment.

She gave him a frigid look as he slid his lean body across the bench next to Gail. Clad in a charcoal gray business suit and white shirt, he looked authoritative and formidably attractive—a perfect complement to Gail's stunning loveliness. When he turned to look warmly at his beautiful companion, Vicki speculated that he had deliberately brought the former beauty queen to show her how little she and last night had meant to him. It was going to be a long hot summer, Vicki thought. Despite all her precautions, Vicki scolded herself, she had once again been duped into a nonprofessional relationship with a man who was in a position to exploit her.

"That looks good," Clay said pointing at Vicki's umbrella-topped banana daiquiri, "but I think I'll pass drinks up and go straight for the food. If you don't mind we'd like to order quickly. Gail and I have an appointment at two."

They complied, quickly ordering Szechuan lo mein, chicken with cashews, and a spicy shrimp dish and agreeing to share them all. The conversation flowed easily as the foursome scooped into the steaming platters heaped with food. Once Vicki and Clay reached for the same morsel of scallop and locked tines. With a start Vicki yanked her fork back, looking up to meet Clay's amused gaze.

"We just have to stop meeting like this," he murmured in his sexy drawl.

Vicki reddened and, attempting to ignore Clay, quickly turned back to Gail and resumed their discussion of the public relations staff's plans for a real Southern ball later this summer.

"I'm envisioning it as a scene straight out of *Gone With the Wind*," Gail said animatedly, her eyes glowing with the romantic vision she was conjuring up. "The women will be dressed in hoop skirts and the men will wear tails. We'll use the grand ballroom in Magnolia House. It will be an occasion I hope people will want to tell their grandchildren about," she declared with a graceful sweep of her hands.

"You're really thinking big," Vicki commented. "That sounds like a lot of work."

"Oh, I don't mind that." Gail shot her a dazzling smile. "I like challenges."

Vicki could believe it, too. Underneath Gail's Southern belle façade, Vicki sensed, lay a strong, capable, and efficient manager. Again she found herself admiring Gail and responding to her charm, but at the same time, Vicki felt inadequate once again. Obviously Gail was a woman who could keep her femininity and handle herself in a man's world. Why couldn't she do the same, Vicki asked, berating herself for her own poor handling of the situation with Clay. Maybe there was no need to warn Gail after all. She seemed perfectly capable of taking care of herself, even around seductive woman traps like Clay.

"We'd better get going," Clay said, looking at his watch. "I've got a couple of things I've got to get done first for the class I'm teaching tonight before Gail and I meet with the governor."

Gail put her elegantly manicured hand on his arm. "Oh, we can't leave until we open our fortune cookies," she said, flapping her long eyelashes at him in mock coyness. "That's always my favorite part of a Chinese meal." Clay grinned indulgently.

Breaking open her cookie like an eager child, Gail pulled out her fortune, reading it aloud. " 'Success will follow your footsteps wherever you wander.' "

"Oh, that was definitely worth hanging around for," she crowed. "I couldn't have gotten a better one if I had written it myself. How about yours, Vicki? What does it say?"

Obediently, Vicki snapped hers open. She smiled as she read the legend, and despite herself, she shot Clay an amused look. " 'Beware of tall dark strangers with honeyed words.' " Oh, I couldn't have done better if I'd written this one myself, she thought, ironically parroting Gail's earlier observation.

"I'd like to stick around and do more crystal ball gazing, but right now Gail and I have to focus on the present," Clay remarkly wryly. Rising to his feet, he peeled off several bills to pay his and Gail's portion of the check and placed them on the table. "I think that should cover us," he said, glancing at Martin.

The other man nodded. "Looks fine," he said, counting the money and then pulling out his own wallet. "I hope your meeting goes well. I'll give you a call later this afternoon, when you get back. There's something I want to hash over with you."

When Gail and Clay, still looking like the perfectly matched couple—she with her cascade of blond curls and he with his romantic dark handsomeness—disappeared out the restaurant door, Vicki started to rise from her seat. But she was only halfway up when Martin forestalled her by placing a stubby hand on her arm.

"If you don't mind, Vicki," he said giving her an appealing look, "I'd like to have a few more minutes of your time. Would you like another cup of tea or a liqueur?"

Vicki arched an eyebrow and then sat down warily. What did he have in mind, she wondered. Refusing the drink, she waited to hear what he had to say. Martin had turned to her and slid his arm familiarly along the top of the leatherette bench behind her. Vicki had to force herself not to draw away.

Is he going to proposition me? Vicki asked herself, taking in the ingratiating smile Loomis was now offering her. Again, to her chagrin, she found she was far from recovered from her earlier experience with Jerry Pratt. The very thought of having to deflect a business associate's sexual overtures made her palms go wet and cold. But she soon discovered that the kind of proposition Martin Loomis had in mind didn't involve bedroom antics.

"I've been watching you at work, and I want to tell you how impressed I am by your technical expertise," he began. "It's really great to meet a gal who can manipulate a technical design like most women can lay out a sewing pattern."

Vicki flinched inwardly. If there was anything she hated it was that kind of patronizing talk about women, even if he did mean to pay her a compliment.

"Thank you," she forced herself to say.

Oblivious to her true thoughts, Martin forged on. "My firm could use women like you. We're a progressive company that wants more technical women. Truly competent females in this field are difficult to find," he said, leaning toward her and looking her straight in the eye. Vicki dismissed his effort to make eye contact as a tactic for expressing sincerity that she suspected she had learned in a management course somewhere. "It's a pleasure to meet a competent woman in computers, and it also doesn't hurt when they're as terrific-looking as you," he said with a wink.

Vicki smiled inwardly and began to prepare a response. She knew now what was coming. Loomis was smoothing his path for a raid on Montgomery's personnel, and she was the targeted victim. In a way she was flattered. After all, it wasn't so long ago that she'd felt she'd be unemployed permanently. It was nice to be wanted no matter who wanted you. But leaving Montgomery Systems to work with a man like Martin Loomis did not interest her. As she listened to his next words, she moved her water glass and traced a damp design on the table with its wet ring.

"I'd like you to come work for us, and I can promise we can offer you an attractive salary. We're so much bigger than Montgomery that we can afford to hire the best people and pay them what they're worth," he said, pausing to take a sip from his tea cup. "What's more, we're a dynamic company, and our growth is so rapid that once you've come aboard we can promise that your chances for quick advancement up the corporate ladder will be excellent."

Vicki nodded. "I'm sure," she said noncommittally.

Leaning closer, Martin started to hammer home his argument. "How does this sound?" he asked her, naming a salary figure almost half again as much as she was making now. Involuntarily her eyes widened, and Martin leaned back with a Cheshire cat smile as he noted her surprised intake of breath. "I thought that might get your attention," he remarked.

"It is generous," Vicki allowed, as she regained her composure. She couldn't dismiss that kind of salary offer so easily. Earning money like that would certainly mean a dramatic change in her life style. She might even be able to buy her own townhouse on the beach, a fantasy she'd been cherishing for years. Travel would be a possibility, too. There would be all kinds of things she could do on a salary like that. On the other hand, she thought, idly pushing a spoon back and forth across the tablecloth, it would mean leaving Ellen and her friends at DDI, and who knows how well she'd get along with a company dominated by aggressive men who were not used to working with women and who might resent being forced to. "You've taken me by surprise," she finally hedged. "I couldn't possibly give you an answer now. I'd need to know much more and do some thinking."

Martin chuckled and nodded his head with a show of understanding. "Of course not," he said patting her hand. "I didn't expect an instant answer. All I ask is that you give it some thought. Feel free to think of questions and ask me anything you want."

"Oh, I will," Vicki agreed. But deep down inside she knew she had already made up her mind. Though the money was a temptation, it wouldn't compensate for the freedom and happiness she had at Montgomery. Her easy camaraderie with her boss and colleagues and her feelings of loyalty for the fledgling company meant too much to her. She liked the fact that she could use her own initiative and not have to go through bureaucratic channels to make a move. In a company the size of Martin's she'd be one of many cogs in a very complex machine. Besides, he was obviously trying to buy her off and sabotage Montgomery's chances for getting this contract. She'd never do anything that would hurt Montgomery Systems. Then a new thought occurred to

Vicki. Maybe Martin's job offer was no more than a ruse to confuse her—to throw her off balance and distract her from her job here. Well, she was not about to let him do that. But how would she handle his question right now?

"I'll think about it," she finally told him with a twinge of guilt. Even if she wasn't going to accept the job, it might be a good idea not to commit herself just yet. Maybe that would keep things from getting too antagonistic and she would learn something about his company's methods in the bargain. Still, when she got up from the table and walked out, she felt a tightness in her chest. Deception of any kind bothered her, and she didn't like playing games—personal or business.

6

~~~~~~~~~~~~~~

Guilty thoughts about her deliberately equivocal answer to Loomis's proposition kept Vicki from giving full concentration to her test plan. Finally, well before five o'clock, she switched off her terminal with a disgusted snap of her wrist and leaned back in her swivel chair.

What are you feeling guilty about, she admonished herself. He's the one who tried to buy you off this contract. You're only trying to find out what his game really is.

The thought strengthened Vicki's resolve. Turning on the machine again, she logged in and tackled her work with new determination. This time the operational guidelines she had been struggling to formulate came together like interlocking words on a game board. And as she proofread her documentation, she marveled at how well it all stood up.

Glancing at her watch, Vicki was surprised to find that it was already after eight. She'd been so absorbed in the work at hand that she hadn't even thought about the time. And now she'd missed the last dinner sitting at Magnolia House. Stretching, she reached around to massage the tight muscles of her lower back. Sitting in one position for so long hadn't done her any good. What she ought to do was go for a walk and then pick up something light at a carry-out.

Grabbing her purse and closing the door behind her, she headed down the hallway. But as she walked past Clay's office, she was stopped short by the sound of children's voices. Children in Clay's office? That seemed unlikely. Yet the high-pitched giggles coming from behind the partially open door couldn't possibly be those of adults.

Her curiosity aroused, Vicki pushed the slightly ajar door open a little further. To her amazement, she saw DDI's dynamic vice-president sitting cross-legged on the floor in front of a personal computer, surrounded by five eager children who looked no older than first or second graders.

"And here's how you can get the computer to make music," Clay was explaining, putting in the command to make the computer play a note. "Ta da," the machine sang out, and the children clapped their hands with glee.

So this was the class he mentioned earlier. She'd pictured him with a group of university students, not first and second graders. Vicki stood for a while watching him work his magic with the kids. He's fantastic with the younger set as well, she realized with surprise. For a few minutes more, she listened to the six and seven year olds' eager questions and smiled at the thoughtful answers Clay gave in return. And when Clay gave a fanciful explanation about the little three-piece band inside the computer she found herself laughing along with the kids.

Then Clay had the children work the computer. First he taught a curly-headed little girl how to push the keys to make the computer play "Twinkle, Twinkle, Little Star." Clay's praise for her success made her freckled face light up with pride, and then immediately four other voices piped up begging to go next. At that moment, Clay looked up and saw Vicki standing there. Their eyes met in a smile.

"Hi," he said cheerfully. "Want to learn how to play music on a computer?"

Vicki smiled and shook her head. "No, too complicated for me," she joked. "See you later," she said, waving goodbye.

As she walked out of the building, Vicki found herself grinning. C. L. Harper never ceased to amaze her. Tonight she'd seen another side to the man—one she had to admit she greatly admired. He'd probably make a great father, she thought with a smile to herself, but he'd be the last to acknowledge that with his hangups about commitments.

After a short turn around the downtown plaza, Vicki stopped in at a little air-conditioned cafe, where she ordered a Greek salad and sat listening appreciatively to the Middle Eastern music, but her mind still wandered back to the scene she had just witnessed. She shook her head. The man was a puzzle.

Clay obviously enjoyed kids, and he certainly cared about people, she thought, remembering the way his face lit up at dinner the other night when he talked about how their new technology would help families and the handicapped. Maybe he just had trouble dealing with women. Well, she thought chewing her last bit of salad, she wasn't about to figure him out tonight. She stretched her arms and yawned. She was tired. For a few minutes more, she sat contentedly listening to the music. It was good to relax for a few minutes, Vicki reflected. In fact, it was almost too much effort to get up and walk the half-mile back to Magnolia House. But finally, when she found herself beginning to nod right there in the restaurant, she forced herself to get up and take her check to the cash register.

As she opened the door of the cafe, a hot, humid blast of air seemed to envelop her. So when she spotted a taxi parked at the edge of the plaza, she decided to splurge on a ride back. But once she had paid the driver and stepped inside her door, she wished that she'd not been in such a hurry to leave the restaurant.

She couldn't believe it possible. Her room was even hotter than the air outside. Crossing to her air conditioner, she fiddled with the controls. The fan seemed to work, but it was only stirring the muggy atmosphere like a blower in a sauna. When she called the front desk to complain, she found that they couldn't send anyone out till the next morning.

Oh, great, Vicki groaned to herself. Crossing back to the window, she pushed it open and peered out into the blackness. But there wasn't even a breeze. How was she ever going to get to sleep? Well, she'd have to give it a try if she was going to be any good at work the next day.

Not wanting to close the draperies and block what little air was coming in the window, Vicki turned off all the lights before stripping down to her panties. Throwing back the covers, she eased herself down onto the sticky sheets and tried to get comfortable. Even her filmy underwear was too much covering.

Her mind kept conjuring up scenes of snow-covered mountains and icy blue lakes. Even the image of her sister Sally's swimming pool surfaced invitingly in her mind. But the tantalizing thoughts did nothing to cool her off. She watched the green numbers on her digital clock chase each other like hamsters on an exercise wheel— only much more slowly. When the readout flashed midnight, she'd had it. There was no question of getting to sleep in this steam room. She might as well take that walk she'd promised herself earlier.

After throwing a light shift over her damp skin and

slipping on a pair of worn moccasins, she eased open the door of her room and peered out into the darkness. There was not a soul about. All she could hear was the contented hum of her neighbor's functioning air-conditioning units.

Glancing up at the main building, Vicki could see that all the lights were also out at Magnolia House. No one else seemed to be up. And so it was probably safe to slip outside for a midnight stroll. Vicki would never have considered such a course in Santa Barbara; it would have been too dangerous to walk by herself at night. But here, everything seemed different.

A little breeze began to ruffle her hair as she padded quietly past the row of doors to her right. The moving air felt good against her heated face. And as the moon came from behind the clouds, she decided to follow a path leading to the interior of the grounds. An iron gate stood open slightly and groaned as she pushed it further. It gave entrance to a little park where the paths were hedged in by ancient boxwoods, their characteristic scent filling the night.

As though looking for an adventure, she hurried along the brick walks, all at once feeling a little like Alice in Wonderland in the garden of the Red Queen. Ahead of her, Vicki heard the sound of splashing water and quickened her step. The brick path ended in a wide open area surrounded by a thick carpet of grass. To her delight, Vicki saw that it sheltered a pool bordered by rocks and shrubs and fed by a cascading waterfall. At one end was a diving board, partially obscured by the shadows. It looked as inviting as the images she had tortured herself with in her oven of a room.

Did she dare take a dip? she wondered, glancing over her shoulder and peering into the shadows cast by the boxwoods. Feeling adventurous, Vicki kicked off her shoes and wiggled her toes in the short cropped grass that bordered the water on all sides, luxuriating in the sudden feeling of freedom the impulsive gesture gave her. Then she walked over to the rock-lined verge of the pool. Scooping up a handful of water, she let it trickle down her face and onto the front of her cotton shift. It felt heavenly. But the uninhibited action suddenly made her self-conscious. And all at once she had the odd sensation that she was being watched.

Slowly she turned her head in all directions, her eyes probing into the shadows at the edges of the bushes and along the sides of the pool. But she could see no one. You're just being silly, she told herself sternly. There's nobody here.

As if to prove to herself that she was right, she turned back to the pool and stuck out a foot, dangling it over the side and making small circles in the clear water. The feel of the cool liquid against her skin seemed to wash away her reservations. With one swift motion, she pulled the shift over her head and tossed it onto the rocks. Like a Venus returning to the sea, she executed a graceful dive off the board and felt herself plunging into the silky water.

Vicki surfaced and threw her head back, letting the water sweep her wet hair out of her eyes. The delicious sensation of cool water on her naked skin made her feel like a sea nymph. Her world had suddenly contracted, and she was oblivious to everything except the enchantment of the crystal pool. Turning on her back, she began to kick her feet in the water, sending a shower of spray into the night air. And then she flipped over on her stomach again and struck off in a strong crawl toward the far end of the pool.

When she reached the edge, she hung on to the rocks at the side for a moment. But just as she was about to push off for another lap, she heard a soft splash to her left. Panicking she clutched the rocks behind her and looked around, trying to figure out what was happening. But there was nothing to see in the darkness except an expanding half-circle of ripples.

Maybe it was time to get out, she told herself, letting out the breath she had been unconsciously holding. But just as she turned to hoist herself up on the rocks, a restraining tug on her ankle pulled her back into the pool. She opened her mouth to scream, but a wet hand promptly thwarted her attempt. Her eyes went wide with fright as she felt herself being turned around in muscular arms. And suddenly she was face to face with a broadly grinning Clay Harper.

"Didn't your mother tell you that midnight swims can be dangerous?" he questioned playfully. "I was taught to use the buddy system myself."

"Buddy system, my foot! What are you doing here?" Vicki sputtered.

"Following you, of course," he admitted with obvious amusement in the face of her rising anger. "I was always partial to skinny dipping."

His words made Vicki suddenly aware that she hadn't a stitch on. And despite the coolness of the water and the darkness of the night, she could feel a hot flush spreading across more than just her face.

It was the wrong moment for the moon to come gliding from behind the clouds, but even Mother Nature seemed anxious to add to her discomfiture now. The only thing Vicki could do was sink lower in the water. And that made Clay laugh with a deep baritone that reverberated off the surface of the pool as though a crowd were in attendance.

"Are you out to attract an audience?" Vicki hissed, trying to pull away from the hand that now held her by the shoulder.

Clay only shook his head. "There's nobody around," he assured her. "Anyhow most of the DDI staff has been moved to their permanent quarters in Stone Mountain

Center so I don't think we have to worry about intruders."

He was right. It wasn't likely that any of the people left at Magnolia House would be strolling around this time of night. The thought quashed her little show of bravado, and the slow, sensual inspection he was now giving her only increased her discomfort.

"I saw you from my window and I had to follow you," her captor murmured softly, almost as if he felt the need to justify his own actions. "Your shift was transparent in the moonlight," he added. "And woman, when your body beckoned me so invitingly to share your midnight adventure, how could I refuse?"

His fingers traced random patterns on her bare shoulders as he leaned to whisper in her ear.

"Besides, you really don't have to worry about us being interrupted. When I followed you down the path, I locked the gate at the entrance to the maze. It only opens from the inside now."

Somehow the thought that they had no chance of being discovered was not all that reassuring.

"You didn't!" she accused.

"Oh, yes I did," Clay confirmed. "And the least you can do after luring me out here is to join me in a moonlight swim."

The challenge was issued with a teasing note intended to relax her guard. Vicki returned his gaze with an accusing look that told him she had no illusion about the danger of accepting his invitation. But ignoring the refusal in her eyes, Clay proceeded to pull her along beside him in a lazy lap of the pool. There was nothing to do but enjoy the moment.

In companionable silence, they floated near the cascading waterfall. Vicki could feel its gentle spray on her face. Even though Clay's arm rested on her shoulders in only casual contact, she felt a shiver of anticipation run through her body.

How could he affect her like this when he was hardly even touching her? It was crazy being alone with Clay in this secluded spot, her mind argued. Anything could happen. Better leave now before it's too late. With that thought in mind, Vicki tried to pull away. But the action seemed to break the playful mood of the last few minutes.

"Surely you aren't leaving yet," he drawled, tightening his grip on her shoulders. "You haven't experienced the best part of a midnight swim."

"Best part?" Vicki said doubtfully.

"Making passionate love in the moonlight, of course." Clay's words were said in a seductive low voice that sent Vicki's pulse racing.

"You wouldn't dare—"

But he cut her protest off with the slow descent of his lips. At the same time, his strong arms pulled her body firmly against his. Vicki was suddenly vividly aware that Clay, too, was not wearing a bathing suit. Bringing up her hands, she tried to push him away, but it was like trying to force back the water that was tumbling over the cascade at the other end of the pool. His lips left hers to slide along the line of her jaw. And then his warm breath fanned her ear.

"Water sprites who indulge themselves at midnight have to be prepared to take the consequences."

"I don't have to take anything," Vicki choked out, still trying desperately to put some distance between herself and Clay Harper. But at the same time, she found herself struggling with her desire to be stroked and caressed by this overpowering man.

"Just relax," he whispered seductively. "Stop fighting me."

In the next moment his mouth had returned to hers, and Vicki felt the insistent pressure of his lips forcing hers open. The rational part of her brain still wanted to resist his attack on her senses. But her body seemed all too ready to surrender to the enemy. Yet, was he really an enemy, after all? She felt his tongue breech the barrier of her teeth and dart into the warmth of her mouth. Without giving the matter any more conscious thought, her own tongue met his in a deep and intimate kiss.

Sensing the strength of her passion, Clay slid his hands slowly down her flanks, the water smoothing their silky descent to her hips. Reaching around to the back of her body, he pulled her firmly against his lower torso. Suddenly Vicki was left in no doubt as to the extent of his arousal. The realization was startling, and once more she stiffened in his arms.

"It's all right. Nothing's going to happen that you don't want to happen," he promised, his hands stroking her body in a way that was comforting, even as his touch continued to excite her.

"I want to believe you," Vicki murmured. "But you're rushing me again."

"The decision is yours. Ask me to stop and I will," Clay countered, pulling slightly away so that he held her body suspended in the water a few inches from his own. As he waited for her answer, his right hand gently began to caress the full curves of her breasts, hardening her nipples to aching points of tension and sending shivers of sensation down through her body.

The decision was hers, Clay had said. But what he was doing with his hands was jumbling her thoughts as well as enflaming her emotions. She had told herself that getting involved with this man was asking for trouble. Every time he touched her, though, all her resolve melted in the fiery passion he could kindle so easily. The havoc Clay was creating with her senses made it difficult to speak. But Vicki knew she had to say her piece.

"Remember what I told you last night," she reminded him. "I'm just not sure."

"If you think this has anything to do with our business contract, you're wrong," Clay insisted. "We're simply two people who are drawn to each other. And I wish like hell I'd met you under other circumstances so I'd be free to make love to you without you reading ulterior motives into every touch and kiss."

With that, his lips claimed her again, and Vicki shivered at the intensity of her response. At the moment it didn't matter whether he was right or not. She might regret this tomorrow, but tonight in this sheltered, intimate environment she felt helpless to stop herself from surrendering to the sensuality of his lovemaking.

The moon cast its silvery radiance around them, shimmering on the water with ethereal, inviting beauty. Even the elements of nature were conspiring to undo her.

Clay seemed to know her decision even before she had fully admitted it to herself. Before she could change her mind, he was guiding her toward the shallow end of the pool, where a molded underwater ledge lay waiting for them.

All the while his hands and lips kept up their erotic attentions, tuning the very core of her femininity to his will. His lips trailed damp little kisses down from the line of her jaw to the nape of her neck. And at the same time, his fingers found her nipples, circling and gently tugging at them until Vicki moaned her exquisite pleasure, running her own hands convulsively over the strong muscles of his shoulders and back. One of his hands left her breasts to stroke the length of her torso and then moved lower still, in an intimate caress that transformed the blood coursing through her veins to liquid fire.

They had reached the underwater shelf at the end of the pool, and Clay seated her on the very edge, parting her legs so that he could stand closely in front of her. The water came only a little above their waists. Bending, Clay swept the tip of his tongue across one breast, licking off the droplets of water that clung to her skin. Then his lips found her nipple, sucking it into his mouth with a gentle force that made Vicki quiver with delight. She bent to press her cheek against the top of his head, running her hands tenderly through the wet thickness of his hair.

"Oh, Clay," she murmured. "I want you so badly."

"Yes," he agreed, lifting his face so that his lips could capture hers in a hungry kiss that transmitted the depth of his need to her.

Instinctively she slid forward, seeking to join their bodies. And then his hands were on her buttocks, guiding her toward him. The velvet tug of the water around them slowed his movements as they came together. At that instant, his passion-dark eyes sought hers, and Vicki thought she might drown in their depths. She cried out her joy as he began to move, still gently at first but then with a rising urgency he was helpless to control.

She felt her own ardor building with his, carrying her to realms of pleasure she had never dreamed possible. Higher and higher they climbed together—each fueling the transport of the other—until the rapture of it was almost unsupportable. She felt his body begin to shudder convulsively, triggering her own reaction. And for a moment out of time they soared together in tremorous ecstacy.

In the aftermath of their passion, Clay pulled Vicki closer, holding her protectively in the circle of his arms. Her head dropped to his shoulder, but she was unable to stay quiescent. What she had experienced with Clay was so much more than the purely physical. She was in love with him, she acknowledged, and she wanted him to know the depth of her feelings. Her lips caressed his shoulder, and her fingers ranged over his back, trying to convey the nearness she felt.

She expected him to speak first, but he remained silent. She waited hopefully for some sign from Clay that he shared her feelings. Finally it was her voice which broke the stillness of the night.

"Clay?" she murmured.

For a long moment Clay did not answer, and Vicki found herself wanting to fill the void with more words. There were so many things she ached to tell him now. But as the silence lengthened, she realized the wisdom in holding back the flow of emotion she had wanted to share with him.

With a little tremor of apprehension, she felt Clay shift his position so that his eyes could meet hers. "Vicki, I know what you're thinking. I care about you. I really do," he said, taking her hand. "But let's keep things in perspective. Let's not get too serious about this. We do have to work together—you were worried about that yourself."

Despite her feelings, she found herself nodding dumbly.

Had she heard him right? she wondered. But the expression on his face made it all too clear that her ears had not been playing some cruel trick. Her gaze dropped, and then she twisted her body out of his grasp. Conflicting emotions of love and anger raged within her. Was this really the man she'd opened herself to—exposing the core of her vulnerability like a tightly curled bud stripped of its protective outer petals? She'd obviously let the paternal scene she'd witnessed earlier that night sway her into thinking Clay might be more than his charming persona suggested. That, along with her traitorous emotions, had certainly led her into playing the fool once again.

Suddenly hot tears stung the backs of her eyes. But she

would not give Clayton Harper the satisfaction of seeing her cry. Quickly she climbed out of the pool, located her shoes and shift in the moonlight, and headed back toward her room. She had been overheated when she had come out into the sultry Georgia evening, but now she was shivering—and not just from cold.

7

Though the damp sticky heat that had driven Vicki out of her room earlier that night had dissipated toward dawn, she still tossed and turned in her narrow bed. There was no question in her mind now that what had happened between her and Clay had been a mistake. But how bad a mistake was it? she asked herself as she shifted her position for the hundredth time and plumped her pillow in frustration.

At first she had only been worried about compromising her professionalism. But there was a more important question now. What was happening to her emotionally, or rather, what was she letting Clay do to her? Once again she told herself she wasn't the sort of girl that would lightly let a man make love to her. She'd given in to sincere emotions of passion and tenderness in those intimate moments with Clay, and now that he'd made it clear that his deeper feelings were not involved, she felt wounded. He was only playing with her, she told herself.

And worse yet, he'd even gone out of his way to warn her about his less than noble intentions. So she had no one but herself to blame for the misery she was going through now.

Vicki stared up at the ceiling with aching eyes and wondered if she was being a big fool and falling in love with the man. If she was, and she already feared she had, then she was in for an even rougher time than she'd had after the Jerry Pratt disaster. For one thing, Clay Harper was not a sensible choice, and also, an outsider like Martin Loomis could easily misinterpret her motives and accuse her of sleeping her way to a successful negotiation of this contract. The realization absolutely horrified her. That was just the sort of tangled mess she'd been determined to avoid. She spent the night conjuring visions of possible accusations from colleagues, and betrayed looks from Ellen. Sleep eluded Vicki totally.

When the morning sun finally filtered in through her window, she greeted it with bleary eyes. Last night's madness now seemed like ancient history. If it weren't for her haggard looks and sluggish, sleep-deprived body, she'd hardly believe that intimate interlude had really happened. But it had. So where did she go from here? she asked herself. And then she laughed grimly as she headed toward the tiny bathroom to shower. Obviously, the first place to go was to work.

Two hours later, dressed in a crisp tan skirt and green blouse, her hair held off her forehead by tortoise shell barrettes, Vicki was once again immersed in the planning of a system that, though formidably complicated, seemed infintely less complex than her muddled personal problems. The office was quiet because Barry had gone directly over to the communications building to supervise installations. So intense was her concentration on her task that when the telephone jangled on her desk she stared at the shrill instrument as though it were totally unfamiliar. Finally picking up the receiver, she was completely jolted back to the real world by the sound of Gail Patterson's melodious tones.

"Hi there," Gail drawled in her appealing accent. "How are y'all doing?"

"Just fine," Vicki replied after a brief hesitation. As far as she knew, Gail probably regarded Clay Harper as private property. Vicki certainly didn't want Gail to know that now she not only was emotionally involved with the man but had made love to him as well. She felt her cheeks heat as she remembered the passion of his crushing kiss and her own tumultuous response. It was a good thing that picture phones weren't standard equipment in DDI's offices.

"Do you have a few minutes?" Gail asked. "Or better yet, could we take a break together this afternoon? You know the old saying about all work and no play."

Vicki stared at the phone in surprise. What did the self-assured blonde want to talk about? Her heart began to beat double time. Had Clay confessed his "little transgression" to the woman he really cared for? And was Gail planning to read Vicki the riot act? She couldn't blame her if she was. Vicki shifted the phone nervously to the other ear. But Gail sounded so friendly, and as far as Vicki could tell, she wasn't the hypocritical type. If she were angry, wouldn't she come across that way now?

Gail's next words allowed Vicki to relax somewhat. "I'm trying to get out a little PR piece on the center, and I'd like to update my information about you and your project. It'll be released to a lot of newspapers, and I want to make sure it's accurate."

"Well, I'll be glad to fill you in," Vicki assured her.

"Then let's combine business with pleasure," Gail continued. "Why don't you let me buy you an iced tea or a lemonade at the Lemon Tree Cafe around three?"

Vicki's relief was so great that she agreed instantly. But some of her guilty fears had resurfaced by the time she approached the cheerful outdoor cafe with its yellow-checked tablecloths and bright yellow and green umbrellas. However, when she caught sight of Gail, who looked fashionably casual in a red cotton sundress that matched the geraniums sprouting from white concrete planters edging the patio, Vicki automatically returned the other woman's sunny greeting. Despite the fact that they were rivals for Clay's affection, it was impossible not to be drawn in by Gail's unpretentious warmth.

"You look tired," the tall blonde observed sympathetically. "I think you women in technical fields must work twice as hard as men." Looking at Vicki with concern in her soft brown eyes, she suggested, "Why don't we get the business part of this meeting over with first, and then we can relax and chat."

Knowing the reason for her exhausted looks, Vicki squirmed. It hadn't been business at all that ruined her sleep the night before. Forbidden pleasure was closer to the mark, she admitted silently, with a heavy dose of morning-after remorse. Wisely, she kept her thoughts to herself.

After ordering iced tea, the two women basked in the pleasant sunshine while Gail scribbled notes on a leather-bound pad. The interview went quickly, but when Gail finally closed her notebook, some of Vicki's apprehension returned. Unconsciously, she began to pleat her napkin into small triangles. What now? she wondered. Did Gail intend to ask her about Clay? And what would her own answer be? She was totally at sea about the status of her relationship with Clay, and she had no clear idea about his involvement with Gail.

Completely oblivious to Vicki's discomfort, Gail rattled on. "I just love outdoor cafes," she offered with a bright smile. "They feel so European. And today's a perfect day for sitting outside. Thank goodness, it's so much cooler than yesterday. If my air conditioning hadn't been going full blast last night, I would have just melted!"

Vicki laced her fingers tightly and mumbled an ambiguous reply. "You're certainly right about the heat." Unlike Gail, she had melted, only it had been in Clay's arms. The young systems analyst shifted in her seat, searching in her mind for a reply that would turn the conversation to a safer subject. Fortunately, at that moment the waiter appeared to offer refills on their drinks.

"I invited Clay to join us," Gail volunteered between sips, "but he said he was too busy."

I'll bet, Vicki thought dryly. But she made no comment.

"That man really does work too hard," Gail declared. "He's a real workaholic like his father."

Vicki lowered her glass and looked up in surprise as Gail continued.

"I swear that boy was born that way. It was probably passed through the genes." Gail set her own glass down and leaned back in her chair.

Vicki felt brave enough to venture a tentative question. "Just how long have you known Clay?" she queried, fearing she might be treading on private territory. Apparently Gail's and Clay's relationship was of long standing, which made her own involvement with the rakish Southerner seem even more tenuous.

"Oh, we were little tykes together," Gail bubbled, confirming Vicki's unhappy thoughts. "We've known each other forever, and we've always been like two peas in a pod." She held up tightly crossed fingers to underline her point. "It's no coincidence we've ended up working for the same company," Gail went on, taking a last sip from her glass. "When DDI made Clay the job offer, he came straight to me and I told him, 'Grab it! It's a great place to work—it's like family here and you'll fit right in.' And I was right. He's perfect for DDI and it's perfect for him." Gail tossed her head and her golden tresses caught the sun and glistened. "We've known each other so long we think alike and we have a lot of the same interests," she continued. "We're both keen tennis players, you know. We've won doubles competitions."

She paused, and Vicki waited for the next blow. So far every word Gail had uttered had seemed like a sword thrust cutting down her fragile hopes. But Gail's next words innocently delivered the coup de grâce.

"What's more we're avid mystery readers and lifelong Willie Nelson fans," Gail went on. "You might think we're twins we have so much in common."

Vicki sorted through this information with a tight feeling in her chest. She was a pathetic tennis player, the kind that serious aficionados sneered at; her favorite reading was science fiction; and, to top it off, she wasn't sure who Willie Nelson was. Vicki's heart sank like a torpedoed ship, and she began to wonder a little desperately how soon she could put this conversation to an end. Nervously, she arranged her skirt while she waited for what she expected would be Gail's next shattering remark.

"We're kin, y'all know," Gail said leaning comfortably toward Vicki. "Cousins. His mother and mine were sisters."

Vicki's jaw dropped. All this time she'd been agonizing over Gail's relationship with Clay. Suddenly her sinking emotions floated buoyantly to the surface.

"You're related?" she asked, her eyebrows shooting upward.

Gail nodded.

"You're cousins," Vicki repeated Gail's statement with a sigh of relief. "You two seemed so close, I thought you were dating."

Gail laughed trillingly. "Oh, no. Clay and I are good buddies. And kin," she emphasized. "I have a boyfriend in Atlanta. His name is Heywood Powell. I call him 'Hey there,' for short," she quipped, leaning toward Vicki and grinning broadly. "He's a journalist with the *Atlanta Constitution*."

Vicki's relief was so great, she was almost speechless. Then Gail shot her a curious look. "Actually," she began a little hesitantly, "I've been thinking there was something like that between you and Clay. I've seen the looks the two of you give each other, and I thought I smelled romance in the air." She reached over and touched Vicki's hand lightly.

Vicki raised a defensive palm and blurted, "Attraction maybe but not a serious romance. Clay's made it clear he doesn't want that sort of involvement."

Suddenly embarrassed by her unthinking outburst, she turned her eyes from Gail's thoughtful scrutiny. All around them people chattered happily in the bright sunlight, and the trees in the planters near the tables cast wavering shadows. But Vicki, in her distress, was blind to the beauty. Involuntarily, she found herself reliving last night's painful scene after their lovemaking. Once more Clay's unfeeling statement, "I'm not interested in commitment," rang in her ears, and she remembered how his blue eyes had iced over as he exchanged fiery passion for a mask of cool indifference.

The two women sat silently for a few minutes, Vicki lost in her inner turmoil and Gail contemplating the remark she intended to make next. "Vicki," she began, pushing a fork and spoon together. "I like you and, of course, I love Clay. I think the two of you would make a great couple and that you would really be good for him." She took a breath as though about to plunge into deep water. "He could use a solid, down-to-earth woman who could keep his feet on the ground. But there's something you should know about him."

Vicki looked up at Gail. The other woman had all her attention now. Was she about to reveal some mystery about Clay that would shed light on his behavior?

"In a lot of ways, Clay is a victim of his own hangups. He's always worried that he takes after his father. And," she sighed, "I'm afraid to some extent he does. Uncle Pat was a workaholic. He blew in and out of his home like a tornado through a cornfield and wreaking just as much havoc at times. He virtually lived at the office or on jet planes en route to business meetings. Poor Aunt Belle, she seldom saw the man, but when they were together all they did was argue about his commitment to the business and his lack of it to his family. As a boy, Clay was caught in the middle," she continued, taking another sip of tea. "He witnessed a lot of stormy arguments between his parents, and one time he vowed to me that he'd never marry. He watched his mother grow bitter, and when his father died so young—he was only forty-five years old, you know," Gail explained, "Clay's negative feelings about mixing marriage with high-powered ambition were confirmed."

Vicki stared at Gail while she tried to take in the entire meaning of her words. Clay's cousin had added a whole new dimension to his personality—one that might explain his avoidance of close emotional ties. Was his family history, as Gail had suggested, the reason? It certainly seemed plausible. Yet there was the man she saw taking obvious delight in instructing the children last night. How could he equate his own love of children with his father's indifference?

Then suddenly a new idea began to take shape in her mind. "Is Clay afraid he's going to die young like his father?" she blurted impulsively.

Gail sat down her glass of iced tea and ran one slender finger over its lip. "Clay has that same unquenchable ambition to get to the top. He's always running around doing things. Even when he's supposed to be relaxing, his mind is on the next project. Many's the ski trip we've taken when Clay's disappeared from our little group sitting in front of the lodge's fireplace, and when one of us has gone to look for him, he's off in his room sketching out a new idea. That boy's just impossible," she added, waving her hand. Then her beautiful face clouded and she began to speak seriously. "I think he identifies very strongly with his father. And since Uncle Pat died so young from a heart attack, I suspect that Cláy fears the same thing will happen to him. That's probably one reason why he's shied away from close, personal relationships with women."

"What do you mean?" Vicki asked, at the same time nodding at the waiter who had refreshed their tea again. Earlier she had been anxious to escape from this meeting. Now she was determined to hear everything Gail had to say.

"I mean," Gail said bluntly, "it's crippled all his relationships with women. Clay plays around with willing ladyfriends but never gets serious because he's probably afraid of getting into a replay of his parents' stormy relationship. And," she continued, lowering her voice to confidential tones, "I do think his fears of dying young like his father may have a lot to do with his attitude. Growing up in the company of a bitter, complaining mother and an absent father really marked him."

Vicki's mind was in a whirl. "But he hasn't come across to me like a workaholic," she stated, thinking of the slow, relaxed Southern charm he'd offered her.

Gail opened her hands out in a gesture of impatience. "He is a carbon copy of Uncle Pat in some ways—he was a handsome devil too—but in a lot of ways Clay is a different man. He may be blind to the fact, but he's really a more sensitive, caring person. And I think the right woman could make a big difference in him. But," she sighed, "I'm afraid he's not going to let anyone close enough to try."

"And his health?" Vicki queried.

Gail didn't answer immediately, and Vicki feared she had overstepped her bounds.

But then the other woman shrugged and said, "As far as I know, Clay is as healthy as a horse. I think he has his mother's sturdy constitution, and I know for a fact he's always careful to eat right and exercise—something Uncle Pat never paid any attention to. But you know," she added with a grimace, "I don't believe Clay has ever seen a doctor for a checkup."

While the sun shimmered down, they sat together in silence for another moment. Most of the afternoon crowd had drifted away, and the tables around them were now empty. Gail looked at the thin gold watch on her wrist. "Oh my, look at the time! I've got to fly. I have a whole slew of meetings to get ready for. This one's on me," said Gail, reaching for the check.

She pulled out her burgundy leather wallet and paid the bill. Then she pushed her chair from the table and rose. Vicki did the same, and together the two young women strolled away from the cafe. When they parted company at the next corner, Vicki was still mulling over Gail's revelations.

"Don't look so glum," Gail exclaimed before turning to go. "I didn't mean to spoil our get-together with such serious talk. Look, the best thing is to take that cousin of mine with a grain of salt. He's fun, but don't fall head over heels in love with the rascal." She flashed Vicki a smile as she headed off in the opposite direction.

But it was an effort for Vicki to smile back. She feared that advice had come too late. Vicki had a lot to think about. And the next day she found that not all of it concerned Clay.

Early the next morning Vicki received a phone call from California. It was Hank with the information Vicki had requested about Martin Loomis.

"That guy's a slick operator," he warned. "So stay on your toes. He's got a reputation of being cutthroat competition. He'll do anything to make a sale."

"Like what?" Vicki asked apprehensively.

Hank's voice lowered to a confidential tone. "Like spreading malicious lies. Rumor is that he won the big Northwood contract by planting innuendoes with a few influential members of the press. He gave them the idea that Ace Electronics, his competitor, was on the verge of bankruptcy. Of course," Hank went on while Vicki's ear was glued to the phone, "he was too smart to soil so much as a pinky of his own grasping hands. He made sure the dirty work was done through a third party."

There was a long silence while Vicki took in her co-worker's explanation. She was glad that Hank had gotten the scoop on Loomis. Unfortunately, however, the information had confirmed her own worst fears. Now she'd have to contend with a man who was about as pleasant and as safe to do business with as a riled rattlesnake. What's more, she'd made herself vulnerable and given him something to strike at. Her foolish midnight tryst with Clay would make a perfect target. If Loomis learned of it, that error in judgment might well be fatal to her career and the reputation of Montgomery Systems.

"Thanks for the information," Vicki told Hank. "The man sounds downright dangerous. Let Ellen know that from here on in, I'll be on guard."

But as she hung up the phone, she remembered Loomis's job offer and her equivocal reply. Maybe it hadn't been a good idea to string him along. In fact, maybe it had been a terrible idea, she thought, unconsciously twisting a strand of auburn hair. Now when she gave him a definite no he might be angry enough to lash out vengefully. She sighed. Who knew what the man might do? And whatever it was, she'd be the one who would have to deal with it. She shook her head as though to clear it. Well, there was no help for it now. She'd just have to give him a definite no as soon as possible.

The opportunity presented itself the following afternoon, when Clay called a meeting to discuss the schedule of events for the center's official opening. On the way into the small auditorium where the meeting was to be held, Martin approached Vicki and tapped her on the shoulder.

"Decided yet?" he asked her with a toothy smile.

Vicki almost had to stop herself from cringing. "Well," she answered hesitantly, putting a hand in the pocket of her cream-colored linen jacket and surveying his smooth face warily, "I'd like to have a word with you after the meeting, if it's all right."

Loomis favored her with a conspiratorial wink and twined his arm familiarly through hers. "Anything that's good for you, is good for me," he said, escorting her down the carpeted aisle and sliding into the upholstered seat next to her.

Vicki felt almost itchy with discomfort. Not only would she have what would turn out to be an unpleasant encounter with him, but she would have to make small talk beforehand until the presentation began. Fortunately, Barry, looking his usual rumpled but friendly self, appeared at that moment and plopped his lanky body down in the seat on Vicki's other side. As he launched into anecdotes about his most recent and quite adventure-filled trip into Atlanta, Vicki was relieved to focus her attention on him so as to avoid further conversation with the threatening man on her right.

Only a few minutes later Clay and Gail walked into the half-filled auditorium and set up the viewgraph along with some charts. Gail looked stunning as usual, Vicki noted. This time she could make the observation with no pangs of jealousy. The tall blonde in her gray tailored suit looked every bit the efficient, confident public relations director and was the perfect complement to Clay's darkly handsome, authoritative presence.

Barry chattered on, but Vicki was almost oblivious to his words now. As though mesmerized, her eyes followed the lean grace of Clay's masculine body as he strolled back and forth across the small stage. His expensively tailored navy suit set off his athlete's physique. As she watched his powerful thighs move beneath the light-weight wool, an involuntary memory of those thighs pinning her to the sides of the moonlit pool at Magnolia House leapt into her mind. The image came close to wrecking her composure as an unwanted heat spread from the most intimate parts of her body. Instinctively she crossed her legs in a tight defensive motion. Her mouth had gone dry, and she moistened her lips with her tongue as she watched Clay stride briskly to the microphone. Since the painful little scene after their lovemaking that night, Clay had been cool to her and had made no move to see her alone. Now she wondered if he ever would.

The feeling that she was being observed made Vicki shoot Martin Loomis a guilty glance. To her dismay she found that his eyes were pinned to her flushed profile. She shifted uncomfortably in her seat. Somehow she had the feeling the man could read her thoughts.

"Do you know what exactly is going to happen here today?" she asked in the hopes of putting him off the scent.

Loomis smiled easily. "Oh, I just think we're going to get a rundown on all the hoopla in store for us this month," he said.

Vicki blinked and then, looking for refuge, turned back to Barry. Though he'd been talking a mile a minute, she'd hardly heard anything he'd said. "I'm sorry," she apologized. "I'm tired and a bit distracted I guess. My mind keeps wandering off to all the things I have to do to get ready for the opening, so I only half heard the end of your account. Want to run it by me again?"

Barry nodded sympathetically. "I know what you mean. My head's been buzzing with details, too."

Once again he took up his narrative and Vicki made

certain she paid attention this time. The bearded young man had just concluded a wacky story of his battle for a parking space with a little old lady in a bright pink Cadillac when Clay signaled to begin the meeting.

The audience quieted immediately, and Vicki settled back to listen to his resonant tones. His opening remarks stressed the importance of the upcoming planned events as an opportunity to attract new investors in the Stone Mountain Project. His words were persuasive and well chosen, and his audience listened with rapt attention. Only once as he spoke did his dark blue eyes rest briefly on Vicki's face. But that one look hit her like a thunderbolt. Embarrassed by her reaction she lowered her eyes to her briefcase. The man was an absolute menace to her composure.

How could he seem so totally cool and professional— as if nothing out of the ordinary had happened between them? Certainly, her mind argued, that couldn't be the case. An episode as wild and passionate as their moonlight encounter had to have left some impression on him, even if he hid behind a "no-commitment" guise. Had he, too, been disturbed when he looked at her? she wondered. And if so, was he deliberately avoiding any more eye contact with her because of it?

Following Clay's remarks, Gail stood at the microphone and in her chatty Southern drawl ran down the schedule of events planned for the VIP's visit.

"That babe's really something," Barry remarked under his breath.

Vicki wrinkled her nose and shot him a half-amused glare. "Sexist," she teased him.

Barry's unabashed admiration of the physical attributes of the opposite sex was an ongoing joke between them. Her installation technician was one of the few men she felt comfortable enough with to banter about the sensitive issue. Barry, like Hank, was an easygoing guy who was happily married and, despite his teasing, never failed to treat women as equals on the job.

"You bet, and then some," he retorted with a mock leer before turning his attention back to Gail's speech. At that point Gail began to close her remarks with a vivid description of her pet project—the Magnolia Ball.

"It will be a real traditional event, and we're asking that everyone dress in period costumes—the gentlemen in cutaways and the ladies in hoop-skirted ballgowns. This is your chance to pretend you're Scarlett O'Hara or Rhett Butler in *Gone With the Wind.* And for those of you who don't cotton to starring roles," she paused grinning at her own pun, "we'd like to see a few Ashleys and Melanies on our dance floor as well." Gail's smile broadened, and there was a rippling of murmured interest in the audience. When it finally died down, she went on to explain that a costume rental company in Atlanta would provide tuxedos and ballgowns. "But get there early," she warned, "or all the best ones will be taken."

As the crowd dispersed, Vicki rose unwillingly from her seat. It was time for the confrontation with Martin. "You go on ahead," she told Barry. "I'll be along in a few minutes. I need to talk to Martin." Though Barry shot her a quizzical look, he was tactful enough not to ask questions.

"See you later," he agreed, heading toward the exit.

Clay and Gail were doing the same, Vicki noted, her eyes wistfully following the handsome couple out the door. For a moment, she wished she could trade places with the blond PR woman. But that's silly, she chided herself. I'm a project manager, not a foolish schoolgirl with a crush on the local football hero, and I better start acting like a professional.

Steeling herself, Vicki turned to Loomis and allowed him to usher her back to his office. When he closed the door behind them, she took a deep breath, squared her shoulders and searched for words that would make her refusal more palatable. "Martin," she plunged in, but before she could get out another word, he cut her off.

"Well, I hope you're going to say yes today. I've already spoken to my boss, and he's eager to put you on our team. In fact, he needs someone to run a new office in San Francisco right away, and he thought your qualifications were perfect for the job." Martin checked his calendar watch. "He'd like to set up an interview within the next few days, if possible. And, you should know," he said pausing for emphasis, "it would mean a higher salary than the one I quoted to you originally."

Vicki swallowed. This was going to be even tougher than she imagined, and she'd been dreading it all morning. How would Ellen handle a situation like this? she asked herself. Ellen would not pussyfoot around, she'd be direct and professional. Vicki took another deep breath.

"Martin," she began once again in a firm voice, "your offer is tempting and I gave it a lot of thought, but I'm afraid I'll have to say no. I think I have a strong future with Montgomery Systems, and my job with them has a lot of growth potential." She stuck her hands in the pockets of her jacket and met his gaze levelly. "It's true my job doesn't have the perks or the salary you're offering, but I like working for a small company. I feel I have a great deal of flexibility at Montgomery, and I'm just not willing to give that up at this stage of my career. But thank you anyhow."

Vicki had forced herself to meet his eyes during this entire speech, and she had watched several expressions cross his face. His look had gone from one of complacency to surprise. But it was the last expression that was giving her qualms. A brief flare of absolute fury had flitted through his narrowed eyes, but quickly he'd covered it with a mask of genial salesmanship.

"I wonder if you've really considered all the angles of the situation. Take a look at all the potential in this job," he insisted with a sweeping gesture of his hand. "With a small company like Montgomery you'll never get the opportunities we can offer. Take—"

But Vicki cut him off. "Martin, thank you, but no," she said flatly. "I've made my decision."

"But—" he protested.

However Vicki had already turned to leave. Now that she'd said her piece, she wanted to beat a hasty retreat. But Loomis had other ideas. As she put her hand on the doorknob, he stopped her by holding the door closed.

"You're going to regret this. And regret it soon," he snarled.

Vicki's green eyes widened in alarm. With a chill she knew he was not just talking about her long-range future; the threat was much more immediate than that. A hint of menace in his voice told her that from now on she'd have to look over her shoulder.

In the days that followed, Vicki's first defensive reaction was to throw herself into the final preparations for the VIP word processing demonstration scheduled that month. Much to her relief, Martin Loomis made no overt move to give her trouble. In fact, she hardly saw him during the next week. However the fact that she had not seen Clay either did little to boost her spirits. She had finally concluded that he'd found other female companionship and that their affair, such as it was, was now ended. Under the circumstances, she couldn't work up much enthusiasm for the approaching ball. Yet when she'd told Gail she'd decided to pass up the event because she had a lot of work to do, the tall blonde insisted that Vicki come.

"Oh, come on now, Vicki," she teased. "Surely, you aren't going to let all this machinery run your life." As she spoke, she gestured impatiently toward the DDI computer room. "Anyhow, I'd like you to come to the ball," she added, looking the redhead in the eye until Vicki nodded her assent. "Now, you make sure you go get a costume that will dazzle everyone."

Reluctantly, Vicki had broken down and agreed. But when she finally did find the time to get to the costumer's in Atlanta, she discovered the selection of dresses had been thoroughly picked over. Gail was right about selecting a gown early, she thought looking ruefully down at what she'd had to settle for—a pale yellow that made her skin look sallow. But what does it matter? she asked herself as she extracted the unsatisfactory gown from the trunk of her borrowed car in front of Magnolia House later that day. Looping the plastic encased outfit over her arm, she turned and almost ran into Clay, who was walking down the broad marble steps of the mansion. Spotting Vicki and her bundle, he paused and doubtfully eyed the dress she carried.

"Yellow, huh?" he remarked as he lifted the plastic to get a better look. Then he took the faded-looking dress from her arm and held it against her. "Doesn't quite do you justice," he said.

Vicki stared up at him in astonishment and then outrage. Why, the man had hardly spoken to her in the last week, and now he was taking it upon himself to criticize her clothes. Snatching the gown away from him, she turned and marched down the path without a backward look.

"You're going to look like Scarlett O'Hara's poor country cousin," he shouted teasingly.

"Poor but respectable," Vicki tossed back at him as she opened the door to her room and then shut it firmly behind her.

8

~~~~~~~~~~~~~~~~

The irritating scene with Clay was still on Vicki's mind as she pulled open the office door early the next morning. Barry, who would be leaving that afternoon for an assignment at Epcot Center in Disney World, was an inveterate tinkerer and perfectionist. He was already at work on the machines in the control center making some last-minute adjustments before his departure. Vicki smiled and shook her head. He never seemed to stop making minute adjustments in the equipment. Often he'd get so involved in working out a bug that he'd miss lunch or forget about eating dinner—omissions that he could hardly afford with his lanky, bordering on skinny, build.

"Been here all night?" she teased, looking at her thin watch and noting the early hour.

"I would have been," Barry told her, "if Bonnie hadn't arrived on the eleven P.M. plane. But when your wife arrives to join you on a special assignment, you make some adjustments. Just remind me to get out of here by eleven thirty so we can catch our plane to Florida. This Epcot thing may be work for me, but it's a vacation for her," he added as he blew at a lock of brown hair that had fallen across his forehead.

"And rightly so," Vicki agreed. "I'll set my watch alarm for you and shoo you out at the first buzz."

Vicki turned back to her desk with a small frown wrinkling her brow. Not only would she miss Barry's lively company, but when he'd gone, she would really be on her own with this project. All the other technical staff had left for another installation last week. If anything went wrong it would be up to her to fix it. Of course, nothing would go wrong, she assured herself. If Barry said everything was running smoothly, then it was. But so much depended on her upcoming demonstration. Still, fretting wouldn't accomplish anything, she admonished herself, settling down to work.

The morning flew by quickly, and by twenty to twelve Barry was on his way to meet his wife. The office was empty except for Vicki. She had opened the brown paper bag she'd picked up at the coffee shop a few minutes earlier and was preparing to go over a report when the office door unexpectedly swung open.

Clay Harper strode in, and Vicki almost dropped the sandwich she'd just unwrapped. Clad in tight-fitting jeans and a cotton knit polo shirt with bands of gray and burgundy, he looked athletic and very handsome. She found herself noting how the short-sleeved shirt accentuated the muscularity of his tanned arms and the broadness of his shoulders.

Taking a deep breath, Vicki looked down and shuffled papers as she tried to calm her flustered reaction to his unexpected appearance. But when she mustered the courage to look up again, she discovered his blue eyes wandering appreciatively over the neat curves of her body. She reddened once again and looked down to make sure all the buttons on her dark blue silk blouse were fastened. This is ridiculous, she told herself. He'd been her lover and seen her naked only days before. Yet, despite their previous intimacy, she felt like a gauche high school girl on her first date.

"Ah, you're dressed perfectly for a picnic," he said, gesturing at the pair of blue slacks she was wearing. "And," he added mischievously, "I just happen to have a picnic lunch in the car. Since the weather's ideal and we're both dressed for the occasion, why don't we play hooky and take the afternoon off? You've been working hard," he added, looking at her cluttered desk. "It wouldn't hurt to have a little fun for a change. We could head out to Stone Mountain Park."

The offer was totally unexpected. Was there ever a man as enigmatic as this one? she asked herself. He went from hot to cold quicker than a water tap. One minute he's pursuing me madly, she thought with irritation. Then he's ignoring me. Then he's teasing me as if he's the boy next door. What was she to make of the man and her relationship with him? That was a question she'd been asking herself for days, and so far no reasonable answer had presented itself.

Unconsciously, Vicki clasped her hands tightly as she struggled with her confusion. But then her visitor shifted his weight and shot her a quizzical look under lifted eyebrows and she realized that now was not the time to try and solve this puzzle. No matter what the answer, Clay was waiting for a reply and she needed to make a decision now. Vicki looked down at her tuna fish sandwich and apple spread out on her paper bag. A picnic lunch, she had to admit, would certainly beat that combination. On the other hand, a woman with sense would refuse this maddening man.

Vicki sighed. But it was too late for that now. She was too deeply involved and too intrigued by Clay Harper to say no. Looking up, she shrugged helplessly. "I hope you have something more exotic than tuna fish."

"Oh, but of course," he answered with a dramatic flourish. "Brie and smoked oysters for an appetizer. Crusty French bread. Roast beef. Grapes and wine," he added, ticking off a luscious-sounding menu on his long bronze fingers. "I stopped off at Philippe's and picked up a few goodies in hopes of luring you away from your work station."

Vicki studied the handsome male before her. It was obvious that he was confident of her agreement. The fact stung her pride. She didn't like him taking her acquiescence for granted. However, he had gone to a lot of trouble to set up a tête-à-tête with her, and she began to wonder what he had in mind. Beneath his rakishly flirtatious façade, she somehow suspected there lay a more serious purpose. He had to be as aware as she of all the loose ends in their relationship. Maybe he intended to tie them up or at least cut the strings. Warily she closed up her lunch bag and put it in a drawer.

"Roast beef and wine definitely has it all over tuna fish and overbrewed coffee, so I'm game," she finally answered, grabbing her purse and pushing back her chair. But as Clay held open the door with a gallant gesture, she shot him another guarded look. What did he really intend for this afternoon? she asked herself again. Well, no matter what it was, she'd just have to play her cards carefully until she found out.

But Clay was in no hurry to reveal his real reasons for the picnic. He made her wait while they strolled past the large granite monolith with its deep relief carvings of General Robert E. Lee, Stonewall Jackson, and Jefferson Davis. He watched appreciatively while Vicki marveled at the awesome monument.

All this time Vicki kept asking herself what was really in Clay's mind. But she didn't find out until after they'd finished nibbling on the Brie, oysters, and roast beef and sat back drinking the fine ruby-colored wine Clay had selected. Now leaning back and listening to the final strains of the afternoon carrillon concert that added to the heady charm of her lunch with Clay, she breathed a sigh of contentment.

"This afternoon has really been a nice change for me," she remarked, "I'm glad you asked me." Silently she added to herself that she wished all her encounters with this man who attracted her so deeply could be as uncomplicated. But as the echoing sounds of the bells died away, the words Clay dropped into the silence between them destroyed Vicki's euphoria.

Clearing his throat and turning to her, he said slowly, "It's high time you and I stopped playing games."

Vicki stiffened but managed somehow to keep her face blank. So her instincts had been right. This outing had a more serious purpose.

"Ever since I met you," he continued, "I've felt like I've been on an emotional rollercoaster." He peered into his wine glass and then gazed out over the lake, his eyes reflecting the blue of the sky with even more intensity than did the water. "That night we made love, Vicki, was a truly incredible experience for me," he said turning once more to the woman who was listening tensely at his side. "I haven't been able to get you out of my mind. And I've realized I probably never will." He took her hand, his thumb rhythmically stroking her slender wrist, and she knew he could probably feel her pulse pounding like a jungle drum. She had an ominous sense of foreboding. All her instincts screamed "danger," and every nerve in her body was keyed for defense.

Clay went on doggedly. "You attract me more than any other woman, and what I'd like to do right now more than anything else is take you in my arms." But despite his words, he put her hand back down on the blanket and turned away again. His voice took on a ragged edge. "It's been hell the last week seeing you and not being able to touch you."

Vicki laced her fingers together tightly. Even with her fear of what he intended to say, she still wanted to smooth away the furrows that were wrinkling his brow and feel the thick vitality of his dark hair. Nevertheless, his tone warned her not to. "The last few days have been pretty uncomfortable for me too," she essayed.

He looked back at her bleakly. "It's my fault, Vicki. I've been neither fair nor honest with you. I've wanted you so much that I've been afraid of losing you if I told you the truth. But now, no matter what the cost, I have to let you know what's in my mind."

And what was that? Vicki asked herself, drawing a deep strangled breath and feeling almost faint with apprehension. Suddenly the sun, which moments before had seemed like a golden kiss on her skin, now licked at her like a merciless flame. "What are you getting at, Clay?" she forced out between trembling lips.

He ran his hand over the rough surface of the wool blanket as though by doing so he could straighten out their own uneven relationship.

"Vicki, when I first met you I told you I wasn't after a permanent relationship, and though it hurts like hell to say it now, that still holds." His blue eyes scanned her face looking for her reaction, but Vicki could only stare blankly while her brain spun. The silence stretched out between them like a taut wire. Then she began to realize what Clay was saying. He didn't really want her. Or at least he didn't really want her the way she wanted him. Vicki felt the blood drain out of her face and shivered despite the heat of the sun. In an attempt to conceal the pain she knew must be there to read in her eyes, she turned away from Clay's probing scrutiny.

"I see," she mumbled tonelessly. He was giving her

the brushoff, and the best thing she could do was to make a hasty exit and return to the sanctuary of her office before she made even more of a fool of herself. Breaking down and crying would just make the situation worse. But when she started to scramble to her feet, Clay rose to his and took her gently by the shoulders.

"Please don't go yet, Vicki. There's more I want to say to you." Looking directly into her tear-bright green eyes, he continued, "If I were the marrying kind I'd be proposing to you right now. But I know myself too well and I care too much for you."

Vicki went cold. This was beginning to sound familiar. The "I don't want to hurt you" bit was such a tired old line. It was a bitter blow to hear this spiel from the man she'd been foolish enough to have fallen in love with. Her eyes freezing into emerald ice, she spat out defensively, "What do you want from me, Clay?"

Clay saw the change immediately and his hands tightened on her shoulders. "I know what you're thinking. But don't shut me out now. Give me a chance to explain," he implored.

"No explanations required," Vicki shot back. "What happened between us was just a lark for me, too. Let's just forget it," she clipped out, averting her head. She was lying through her teeth, but there seemed nothing else to do. It was better to end this quickly and not prolong the agony.

But Clay wasn't going to allow that. Swiveling her back to him, he curled his strong fingers around her chin. "You know quite well that it wasn't only a lark for you or for me," he insisted gruffly. "I really care about you. I care about you so much that I'm bleeding inside. I want you and I need you," he groaned, dropping his hand and turning abruptly away from her. "Sometimes I feel very lonely, but that feeling goes away when I'm with you. You're good for me in so many ways."

Even through the tears she was repressing, she noted

the tensed muscles in his neck and shoulders. They testified to the whirlwind of his conflicting emotions.

"But I know I'm no good for you," he added as he stared out over the azure water. He took a deep breath and set his chin as if to ward off a blow. Jamming his hands in his jeans pockets, he continued, "I'm not the kind of guy who can make a woman happy. I'm a self-centered workaholic like my father." Shooting her a defiant look over his shoulder, he went on, "If you stuck with me, you'd end up hating me as much as my mother hated my old man and I couldn't bear that."

"I could never hate you, Clay," she said softly, stepping forward and touching his shoulder. But when he didn't respond, her hand dropped away.

"We're both adults, Vicki," he ground out, facing her. "We both know there's more to a relationship than mutual attraction. Love has its limitations and it can't survive years of neglect. I couldn't provide you with stability. I know myself well enough. I'd always be flying off on some new project. You'd spend a lot of lonely nights. And you'd be right to resent me for it. You'd probably only end up consoling yourself with another man anyhow," he finished gruffly.

It was too much like adding insult to injury. Vicki put her hands on her hips. "Now just wait one minute, Clay. You underestimate me. You're not the only one here with an interesting career. What makes you think I'd be sitting at home crying while you're out conquering the world?" Vicki's hand shot up in an expression of contempt. "I'm quite aware of how the business world works, and I believe I've learned to deal with it successfully. I wouldn't want to be married to a man who expected me to sit around and pine for him." Her eyes flashed at him like warning signals, but as Clay absorbed the challenge in her expression, his jaw only hardened.

He took a deep breath and then plunged ahead. Vicki had the feeling that he had to utter his next words quickly

if he was to say them at all. "Maybe you wouldn't want
the kind of man who'd need a traditional wife. But you
wouldn't want a husband who was going to drop dead in
ten years either, would you," he stated flatly.

Vicki's mouth fell open. Gail had hinted this might be
Clay's problem. But hearing it from him was a shock.
"What's that supposed to mean?"

"Just what I said," he returned starkly. "I told you I'm
just like my old man, and I'll probably end up dying of a
heart attack at forty-five just like he did. So you see I
haven't a lot of time." Stepping forward, he seized her
elbow to guide her to the path leading to the parking lot.
But Vicki wasn't going to be so easily managed. Rebel-
liously, she dragged her feet. Now that his motives were
out in the open, Vicki wasn't sure how to react. Part of
her wanted to argue with him, tell him how ridiculous she
thought his preconceived notions were. Yet at the same
time, she could see how deeply they were imbedded in
Clay's attitude toward love and marriage. Would arguing
with him now only alienate him completely? But this time
caution didn't win out. Vicki discovered she was a fighter
after all. She loved this man, she told herself, and she
wanted him. If he had told her he didn't care for her, she
would have walked away. But that wasn't the message
he'd delivered. Here he was telling her that he cared. But
did he really? Or was he just ducking out of that
commitment with excuses that, as far as Vicki was
concerned, wouldn't stand up under scrutiny.

While Vicki was debating with herself, they broke
through the screen of trees that sheltered the parking lot.
As they got to the gray sports car, she decisively blocked
his move to open the door. Whirling around and facing
him, Vicki charged, "You look pretty sturdy to me." Then
casting him a defiant look she added, "You know what,
Clay Harper? I think you're just copping out. This whole
heart attack business is a convenient excuse." She
paused to let her words sink in. Then, despite the angry

flush creeping up Clay's neck, Vicki persisted. "I'll bet you haven't even been to a doctor. Have you!"

"No, I haven't and I don't intend to," Clay retorted, opening the car door and thrusting her in.

"You're behaving like a child," she accused, staring at his grim profile as he got in on the other side and jammed the key into the ignition. Ignoring her, Clay shifted roughly into reverse and swung the car around, scattering gravel beneath the wheels as he pulled out of the lot. He was obviously angry, but Vicki had gone too far to back down now. "And," she added belligerently, "I bet a doctor would tell you your problem is in your mind, not in your body."

Clay's face was closed. "I don't want to talk about it," he snapped.

"No, you don't want to shatter your precious illusions. They protect you from getting close to people. You're the type of person who'd rather play games, personal as well as those confounded computer games you've invented."

She could see an angry muscle jumping in Clay's locked jaw, but he didn't reply. Vicki folded her arms tightly across her chest and stared blindly out the windshield. It was obvious that she'd wasted her breath. Clay Harper wasn't interested in hearing anything she had to say. They drove the rest of the way back to the office in a stormy silence.

All the next week, while she prepared for the VIP visit, the storm clouds hovered over Vicki's head. Even Barry's postcards with their humorous inscriptions and their inviting pictures of Disney World failed to lighten her mood. Since their confrontation at Stone Mountain Park, Clay had withdrawn into another shell. On the few occasions when he and Vicki had met that week, he had avoided her eyes, and she'd begun to feel that it was all over between them. The thought was so depressing that she had to talk to someone. She called Sally just to ask how things were and hear the sound of a familiar voice.

But Vicki hadn't really come to terms with her shattered romance. She'd been so frantically busy with last-minute details for the opening that she'd pushed her feelings about Clay and his maddening attitude to one side.

The night of the ball Vicki worked late in the office, sorting out papers. Though she knew it was past time to get ready for the dance, at the moment she didn't feel fit for human company, and she certainly wasn't up to the hours of forced gaiety and idle chitchat that the affair would require. Gail, however, had made her promise to make a showing.

"Remember what I told you about all work and no play," the sleek blonde had teased lightly. "Besides, all the important people will be there and you owe it to your company to turn up."

Vicki had to admit Gail was right. She would go, but it would be just for a few minutes, she told herself as she walked back to her room. Planning to take a quick shower, fix her hair, and get dressed, she grimaced as she pictured herself in the faded confection she'd gotten stuck with at the costumer's. Well, hopefully the room would be dimly lit so no one would pay attention to the dress, she thought as she turned the key in the lock.

Walking through the doorway, she looked over at the bed and then halted abruptly and stood gaping in astonishment. There spread out before her eyes lay an emerald satin ballgown that would have made Scarlett O'Hara green with envy. With its full skirt gathered into flounces at the hemline and its bustier bodice with flirtatious puffed sleeves, it was designed to set off to perfection a girl with Vicki's vibrant redheaded looks. Hesitantly she approached it, wondering who had put it on her bed. Someone must have made a mistake and delivered it to the wrong room, she thought unwillingly. Having seen the dress she couldn't bear to give it up. But then her eyes discovered the note lying next to the red rose tucked in the gown's top. Reaching for the paper, she pulled it open, her eyes widening as she read the message aloud.

"You were meant to glow with the beauty of an emerald. Save a dance for me. Clay." Currents of excitement began to course through Vicki's veins. But at the same time, she found the message so bewildering and the act so unaccountable that she reread the words several times, looking for a clue to their real meaning. Why had Clay done this, especially after the harsh words that had passed between them? Vicki sat down on the bed and fingered the gown's fine material. It was the most beautiful dress she'd ever seen. What had moved Clay to do this? Was it a peace offering and would tonight bring a reconciliation? She broke into a hopeful smile, her gray mood radically altered. With quick light movements she began stripping off her office clothes to shower and change for what she anticipated might be an evening to remember.

But even as she admired her transformed image in the mirror a half-hour later, a dark thought sobered her expression. Was she being set up for another fall? How often in the past had she thought that things were smooth between herself and Clay Harper only to be tripped up by his inscrutable behavior?

With flutters of nervousness in her chest, Vicki opened the door and lifted her skirts to glide down the path toward Magnolia House. As she approached the curved driveway, her eyes widened in delight to find the black-topped lane around the mansion lined with shiny black coaches and horse-drawn phaetons in various shades from pale yellow to burgundy and gray. The soft glow of electrified candles and the strains of an orchestra playing waltzes filtered through Magnolia House's Palladian windows. As the music reached her ears, her imagination conjured up pictures of whirling couples. She hastened her step.

At the door a red-coated valet ushered her in, and as

she passed through the red-carpeted hallway leading to the ballroom, another elegantly garbed servant announced her arrival in ringing tones. Drawing in her breath, Vicki stood taking in the brilliant scene. The whole experience resembled a childhood fantasy come true. Gail's skill in pulling this event off was truly impressive. Everything down to the string orchestra, the gleaming chandeliers, and the engraved matchbooks on each table attested to Gail's perfectionism. She had truly recreated a period Southern ball.

Surveying the ballroom, Vicki felt as if she had stepped into an earlier century. It was as though her businesslike twentieth century persona were melting away in the candlelight. For this evening, she resolved, her romantic, feminine inner self would take over. With her hair framing her face in soft ringlets and the satin of her dress swishing around her ankles as she floated into the sea of smiling faces waiting to greet her, she felt the world of computers, contracts, and conflicts fade away.

"Don't you look like the Southern belle tonight?" Gail exclaimed, moving forward and taking her hand. "I'd like you to meet my friend Heywood," she added, bringing forward a tall sandy-haired Southerner. When the introductions were made, Gail gestured at the sweeping skirt of Vicki's gown. "I declare that's the most gorgeous dress I've ever seen in my life, and that green is so perfect on you."

Vicki returned Gail's sparkling look with a wide smile. "You look pretty spectacular yourself." It was the truth. Gail was decked out in a royal blue gown sprigged with pink rosebuds, and her golden hair was caught in an elaborate upsweep and crowned with a jeweled tiara.

"Just wait until my devil of a cousin gets a peek at you," she threatened with a wink. "And wait till you see him. Rhett Butler pales by comparison."

Involuntarily, Vicki found herself searching the ballroom for a glimpse of Clay. The orchestra had struck up a spirited Confederate tune, and the couples on the dance floor made exuberant attempts to keep time with it. Yet, though she scanned the dancers carefully, the handsome vice-president was not among them. However Loomis wasn't in sight either, she noted with relief.

Just as she had given up the search for Clay, she felt two strong hands clasp her waist and warm breath feather her ear. "I see Scarlett O'Hara's beautiful rival came instead of her poor step-cousin," a vibrantly low voice teased.

Startled Vicki whirled around and faced an incredibly dashing Clay Harper. Dressed in a dark cutaway, white ruffled shirt, and string tie, he was the perfect Southern hero. With his mustache, bronzed skin, and deep blue eyes, he was the handsomest man she'd ever seen. And now that those deep blue eyes were twinkling wickedly down at her, she felt little currents of electricity begin to shoot through her veins again.

Lifting his gaze from Vicki's flushed face and looking up at Gail, Clay drawled, "Do you mind if I break up this little chat and sweep this lovely lady 'round the floor?"

"Of course not," Gail said, playfully tapping his hand with her fan. "But you take good care of her, you hear now?" she added over her shoulder as she picked up her taffeta skirt and swished away.

"Oh, I intend to take very good care of Vicki tonight," Clay answered with a mischievous grin as he took Vicki's elbow and led her onto the dance floor.

The orchestra had slowed its tempo to a dreamy waltz, and as Clay put his arm around Vicki's waist and took her hand, she couldn't control the involuntary shiver that ran down her spine. Once again, she had the strange feeling that this night was an experience out of time. She felt like a nineteenth century Southern belle, and Clay was the dashing beau who would ultimately claim her hand. In an instant Vicki dismissed that last thought. She was fantasizing again.

But her partner's next words recaptured the spell she was under. "I've been aching to hold you in my arms all day," he whispered in her ear.

As they revolved slowly in time to the soft music, his warm hand began to stroke her back, and she found herself pressed closer to his body. They didn't speak for a while, and Vicki closed her eyes, drinking in the closeness of his vital male presence. When he did speak again, it was in a husky whisper.

"You look absolutely ravishing in green. I knew the dress would look good on you. But," he added with an admiring smile, "with your gorgeous red hair and the emerald of your eyes, you bring out the beauty of the dress."

Vicki's heart fluttered with pleasure. "It's the most beautiful gown I've ever seen. How did you ever get it? All the costumer's had when I got there, as you may remember, was that tacky yellow thing I brought home."

Clay chuckled and then nipped lightly at her ear. "I pulled a few strings. I had the gown flown in from Charleston."

His hand pressed her slender back firmly against his hard lean body, and they seemed to melt together. Vicki closed her eyes again and enjoyed the sensation of being in his arms. If he had ached for her, she had been aching for him too, and dancing like this was an exquisite torment. There was a sweet frustration about it. The closer he held her, the closer she wanted to be. How would this evening end? she wondered. And what were the other people on the dance floor making of the way Clay was holding her? She knew they must look like lovers, but she wouldn't think about that now. She'd just enjoy the moment.

For the rest of the evening she was lost in a dreamlike

haze of romance. Though she danced several times with
other men and sat and talked to some of the other Stone
Mountain workers, everything that night was overshad-
owed by the moments she spent with Clay. They danced
again and again. When it was time to eat, he filled her
plate at the buffet, teasing her lightly about eating enough
to keep her strength up. He intended, he told her, to
keep her dancing all night.

But later on as they walked out on the terrace for a
breath of fresh air, Clay whispered in her ear, "Let's slip
away and take a carriage ride." He was standing very
close to her in the scented air, and she felt almost giddy
with excitement. Maybe he'd changed his mind about
their relationship. Everything he'd said and done tonight
certainly pointed that way. And if they got away from this
crowd, perhaps he would speak to her about it.

"A carriage ride sounds wonderful," she agreed. "But
where do we hire one?"

"I've already taken care of that," Clay promised, as he
led her down the terrace steps to the brick path that
wound around the house to the driveway.

A few minutes later their open carriage, driven by a
liveried coachman, was swaying gently on the bridle path
that meandered through the estate, and Vicki was cud-
dling in Clay's strong arms. Overhead, the moon filtered
down through the lacy pattern of branches overhanging
the path, shedding a silvery radiance over the carriage
and the nestling couple. She closed her eyes and listened
to the rhythmic clip-clop of the horse's hooves on the
packed dirt. The cool, pine-scented air began to chill
Vicki's bare arms, and she shivered slightly.

"Cold?" Clay asked. When she nodded, he pulled off
his jacket and wrapped it around the both of them,
holding her even more tightly in his arms.

"With your eyes closed like that you look like an
angel," Clay murmured. "And I've always wanted to kiss

an angel." Vicki lifted her moon-silvered face. His head bent and his lips began to brush her mouth softly. "Mmmm, that tastes good."

"And what do angels taste like?" Vicki breathed.

"Like angel food cake. What else?" he whispered, fastening his lips on hers so she couldn't ask any more questions.

Then, what had started as playful caresses began to deepen, and Vicki felt herself responding to Clay's building ardor. Her fingers began to twine themselves in his thick hair, feeling with pleasure the strong molding of his neck. It was so good to be in the circle of his arms, and the flames of her own passion were now flickering to life. Fired by his kisses she moaned softly, "Oh, Clay, what are you doing to me?"

"Shhh," he admonished gently. His lips teased her lashes, and once again she shut her eyes, savoring the delicious feel of his slow seduction. His lips brushed her eyelids and trailed tiny kisses down her cheek. Vicki quivered. Even the feel of the rough texture of his jacket and its buttons pressing through the fine material of her bodice was exciting to her, and in response she pressed her body hungrily to his.

Clay lifted his face from hers and studied her for a moment. "You have the most beautiful long lashes. In this light they're casting shadows on your skin," he crooned, stroking them delicately with his fingertips.

Vicki trembled again, but she didn't open her eyes. She was captured by the fantasy she was living. The sorcery of his lovemaking had woven a magic web around her. And she was unwilling to disturb its fragile beauty. Caught up in that delicate trance, they rode through the warm Southern night.

Even when the carriage pulled up to the door outside Vicki's room, the enchantment lingered. As the beat of the horse's hooves came to a stop, Vicki reluctantly raised her eyelids. Clay's face was bent over hers, a tender smile on his mouth. "Time to take Lady Scarlett home."

As he grasped her small hand to help her from the carriage, Vicki said with playful naivete, "Home to Tara?"

Unexpectedly, he swept her up into his strong arms and she clung to his neck in delighted surprise. After the coachman discreetly pulled away, Clay grinned wickedly down into her shimmering emerald eyes. "Home to bed," he whispered with masculine seduction.

All of her earlier resolve to deny her bed to him melted in the smoky desire that was curling through her body. Studying the strong line of his chin, she released one hand from around his neck and stroked his jaw and lips lightly. "Why Mr. Rhett Butler, I do declare you've swept me off my feet," she confessed, counterfeiting a Southern accent as Clay strode up the stairs and shouldered open the door.

The tempo of life here had been so easy that Vicki never bothered to lock up if she was only going to Magnolia House, so the barrier to her bedroom offered no resistance. Vicki was beyond resistance, too. Kicking the door shut behind them, Clay placed Vicki on her feet, and as she stood giddy with excitement and desire before him, he ran his hands sensually down the line of her slender body. Then drawing her to his hard length, he pressed his lips to hers, embracing them with a passionate kiss.

Up until this moment he had used gentle persuasion, but now his kiss was hungry and demanding. Like a banked fire bursting into flames, Vicki met his urgency. On the carriage ride, she'd been afraid to move, afraid to disturb the fragile beauty of the night. But now, all the yearning that had been smoldering inside her leapt up. She wanted him with an intensity that was making her tremble. There was no way she could deny that. And there was no question that Clay desired her with equal ardor.

"I want to feel your skin next to mine, Vicki," he demanded huskily. Deftly his fingers unhooked the back of her dress and slid the zipper down to the soft feminine swell of her buttocks. Easily, the dress slid with a silken swish to the floor around her silver slippers.

"Oh, I like that," he murmured thickly, his eyes taking in the white lacy corselet she'd worn under her gown. Out of its half-cups, her creamy breasts rose in rounded globes, and his head bent so that his lips nuzzled the soft skin. Unconsciously, Vicki arched her back, pressing the sensitive flesh harder against him. Pushing down the cups to free her breasts, he caressed their fullness, stroking them until they ached with arousal. She felt the prickle of his mustache as he took a nipple between his lips and she wriggled beneath the tantalizing flicks of his tongue. Teasing the pink nipples to an erotic tautness, he began with almost maddening slowness to undo the fastenings of the corselet. So much did she want him that, when the confining garment was finally removed, Vicki was clinging to Clay with mindless need.

He buried his face between the quivering cleavage of her breasts. "My god, Vicki," he breathed raggedly, "you're so beautiful. For days, I've thought of nothing but touching you like this." Tugging at his string tie and pulling it from his collar, he ordered thickly, "Help me get out of my clothes."

Obediently, with trembling fingers, Vicki complied. Moments later, Clay's muscular body was as naked as hers. She stood back and looked at him while he watched her with dark hungry eyes. Marveling at the strength of his manhood, Vicki ran her hands down the length of his taut flanks, stroking the hard sinew and firm flesh. How could he doubt the health of his magnificent body? she wondered. Tenderly, she moved her hand up to his wide back. No woman, not even Scarlett O'Hara, could ask for a more handsome lover. As her hands slipped once more to his muscled buttocks, she felt him surging against the soft flesh of her stomach. And once more she felt the sharp delicious ache of her womanhood's answer to the imperative summons of his male desire.

"Vicki, come to the bed," he insisted in a passion-drugged voice. Again, Vicki felt herself scooped up into his arms and carried swiftly across the room.

As Clay set her gently on the quilted coverlet, Vicki looked up into his darkly flushed face, her eyes brilliant with the glow of love. At this moment she needed Clay more than anyone else in the world. He had only to ask and she would give him whatever he wanted. But Clay was not ready yet to make the ultimate demand. Kneeling over her, he began to caress the silkiness of her stomach with slow and deliberate circular motions of his tongue, and she moaned in sensual delight as his lips slipped to the voluptuous curve of her thighs. When he began to tease the delicate flesh there, Vicki trembled.

"You're opening like a flower for me, Vicki. And I must sample your honey," he murmured.

"Oh, Clay. Please make love to me," she pleaded. "I want you right now."

"Oh yes, Vicki," he answered, lowering his body onto hers. Pulling her buttocks toward him, he filled her liquid core completely so that she cried out in pleasure. As his driving manhood lifted her to height after height of exquisite feelings, Vicki cried out softly again and again. It seemed that as he bore her to each new plateau of ecstasy, she thought there could be nothing beyond each peak. But Clay taught her otherwise. It was not until she had been spiraled off into a new paradise of sensation that Clay finally took his own pleasure.

"Oh, Vicki," he sighed as his now relaxed body covered hers. "You're as much woman as any man could ever ask for," he said, tenderly kissing her heated features. Seizing his hair between her hands, she drew his lips to hers and embraced them with loving sweetness.

When he finally rolled away, he pulled her to him, sheltering her in his arms so that their bodies seemed to be joined once again. Vicki, lost in the honeyed feelings engendered by their lovemaking, clung to his damp form, savoring the feel of his fine masculine physique.

I love this man, she thought as her eyes drifted over the hair-sprinkled contours of his chest and the firmly muscled line of his legs. He was beautiful, and her heart felt almost wrenched with need as he lay quietly next to her. She had to tell him how she felt. She couldn't hold it inside any longer. Surely, he must feel the same way too, she told herself.

"I love you, Clay," she whispered, stroking his cheek.

Clay didn't answer and a sudden fear began to trickle through Vicki's veins like ice water. Her heart began thudding in her chest so hard that it hurt. Unconsciously, she began massaging the flesh of his shoulder as if doing so would bring forth the response she wanted and needed to hear. But he remained quiet, staring up at the ceiling, and a moment later he shifted away.

Still not looking at her, he began to speak in a strained voice. "Vicki, I care about you more than any other woman. But I told you I can't get serious." Then turning to her he added, "You know the reason why."

She stared at him in disbelief, her whole body going icy. Convulsively, she reached down and clutched at the quilt in an attempt to cover her nakedness. Rolling away with her back to him, she felt tears begin to sting her eyes. After what they had shared, his words were like sharp steel plunged into her heart. Once again he had retreated behind the wall of his own fears, and again she felt powerless to break it down. And she would never try again, she told herself bitterly.

9

It's my own wishful thinking that's gotten me into this mess with Clay, Vicki admitted to herself the next morning, staring in the mirror at her haunted eyes ringed with dark circles. I want so much for everything to work out between the two of us that I keep hoping he feels the way I do. But he doesn't. Face it. He can't. That's been perfectly obvious after every time we've made love. He's attracted to me, all right. But for him it's nothing more than a physical passion.

How ironic, she thought, laughing in self-deprecation. Three months ago I was worried because I wouldn't let myself care about someone like Clay. Well, I'm over that hurdle, all right. And where has it gotten me?

Vicki shook her head sadly, thinking about the tangled mess her life had become. This was so very different from what had happened with Jerry Pratt. All the pressure had come from his side. And when she had refused to sleep with him, he'd gotten nasty. But face it, with Jerry, she hadn't even been tempted.

This time, she hadn't been able to stop herself from falling right into Clay's open arms. When he was making love to her, she couldn't think about anything except the exquisite feel of his warm caress. The thought of his teasing hands arousing her body was enough to make her shiver even now.

His lovemaking had meant more to her than just physical passion. She knew that given the chance their relationship could grow and blossom into something very precious. But Clay refused to give the two of them that chance. He had made it clear that she was not included in his future—just his present. And yet, part of Vicki's mind still refused to believe that assessment. It was more than that, she told herself desperately, hoping that she could make it be true.

But what about Clay's callous reaction to her declaration of love? another part of her mind argued, her face reflecting the agony that she was feeling. He'd let her make a fool of herself again and then retreated behind his own senseless hangups. Try as she might to see things differently, in the cold light of morning, her common sense told her that the best thing she could do would be to go back to California as soon as this contract was over and try to erase Clay Harper from her memory.

That was excellent advice. Yet the prospect of taking it made Vicki feel worse than ever. Like a programmed robot she tried to remove all reminders of the last night's disaster from her room. The elegant gown he'd provided would have to be returned, of course. But as Vicki smoothed the fragile material and repackaged the gown in its protective covering, she couldn't help remembering the way Clay's eyes had deepened with admiration when he'd first seen her in it at the ball.

Was she going to spend the rest of her life mooning over the man? she asked herself, hanging the dress up in the closet and firmly shutting the louvered door. No, she decided, clenching her fists with determination. She had more important things to do than torture herself with thoughts of the rakish Southerner who had hopelessly captured her heart.

The big word processing demonstration that would help decide the outcome of the DDI contract award was scheduled for tomorrow. And no matter what, she couldn't let her personal feelings interfere with her job responsibilities. Even though it was Sunday, she felt compelled to go in and check everything out one last time. This contract was just too important to leave anything to chance. And besides, Vicki admitted to herself, she needed something to get her mind off her painful relationship with Clay. Letting her thoughts spin round and round like a whirligig out of control was only giving her a headache.

After a quick shower, Vicki got dressed for work. As on her first day at Stone Mountain, she selected jeans and a Western shirt. I might as well be comfortable, she decided, pulling on the casual attire. Since it was already noon, she had lunch and then walked over to the DDI building.

I wish Barry were here, she sighed to herself as she headed across the orchard toward the DDI building. But unfortunately, Ellen had only been able to spare her ace technician team for the system's installation and initial testing. The tests had gone amazingly well, and Vicki tried to tell herself there wasn't much that could go wrong now. However, she knew from past experience that things were likely to go wrong with computer systems when you least expected trouble.

Because of weekend security, Vicki had to enter through the main computer complex. There was a gloomy, depressing air about the deserted facility. Only one operator, a short, wiry young man with an adolescent complexion and untidy brown hair, was on duty. As she pulled the door open, he jumped and the magazine he had been reading slid off his lap.

"Sorry, I didn't mean to startle you," Vicki apologized.

"What are you doing here on Sunday?" he challenged. "Only certain personnel are authorized for after-hours access."

Vicki fished in her wallet for her DDI contractor identification and then handed it to the operator.

"Well, I guess it's okay," he admitted grudgingly, after studying the card for a full minute. "But don't expect any hand holding from me. I'm busy."

You sure look like it, Vicki thought to herself, wondering just why this young man was going out of his way to be unpleasant. But she wouldn't let his rudeness keep her from doing her job.

"Is the main system up?" she inquired politely.

"Guess so," he mumbled, "but you'll have to answer any console error messages you create yourself."

Vicki shrugged, hoping there wouldn't be any problems. "Okay," she agreed.

Her footsteps echoed hollowly on the raised tile floor as she crossed the area where Barry had set up the terminals. After opening the door to her office, she flipped on the light. But the cold fluorescent radiance did little to cheer up the empty room.

Sitting down at her terminal, she logged in and then began to run a diagnostic program to test the system's capabilities. First she sent some sample correspondence to the main computer for storage. That test seemed to go fine, and she breathed a small sigh of relief. But her relief was short-lived. When she tried to retrieve the original text and edit it at her terminal, strange things started happening. Her cursor, the little blinking light that showed where she was in the text, started bouncing around her CRT screen like a Mexican jumping bean. When she pressed the reset button, the problem seemed to disappear for a few minutes. And then with no warning her cursor was off again, as if it had a mind of its own.

Vicki glanced up, trying to quell the sensation of panic that was rising in her chest. If this happened tomorrow during the demonstration, her chances of winning this competition for Montgomery would be about the same as taking a flying leap off Stone Mountain and landing safely. Just stay calm, she told herself, looking across the dimly lit room at the lone computer operator still reading his magazine.

As she watched, his head lifted from his magazine, and he stared at the console screen in front of him. She saw his brows furrow, and then he glanced accusingly at her. He must be receiving a barrage of error messages at the main console, she reasoned, getting up from her own seat and crossing the room toward him. Fleetingly, she wondered why this was happening now of all times, but getting the system back in working order was her top priority, and that question would have to wait until later.

When she reached the main computer room, the operator was ready with an angry question. "What the hell are you trying to do? I'm going to have to take the whole system down now and reload it to get rid of your error messages."

"I can't imagine what the problem is," Vicki began to apologize, but he was too wound up to listen.

"I've been babysitting this system while it ran through the payroll program. It was almost finished. But now I have to restart the whole thing or nobody around here's going to get paid this week."

"What about my testing?" Vicki questioned.

But he waved his hand in a gesture of dismissal. "I'll be here to midnight if you keep crashing the system, and I've got a date this evening. You're just going to have to wait till the regular shift comes on tomorrow."

"Tomorrow will be too late," Vicki protested. But despite her intent to sound authoritative, a slight quiver in her voice betrayed the panic rising in her chest.

"That's tough," the young man countered. "Now let me boot this thing back up."

Shoulders tense with impotent anger, Vicki stalked

back to her office. She'd known some indifferent computer operators in her time, but this guy took the cake. Evidently he wasn't going to listen to anyone unless they had direct authority over him.

Pacing back and forth, she tried to remember the name of the operations chief she'd met last week. But when it came to her it was less than useless. Just my luck, a Smith, she sighed. The only other person who might be able to help was Clay. And she certainly didn't want to call him after the disastrous way their night together had ended. But after forty-five minutes of considering and discarding a dozen other alternatives, she picked up the phone and called his room at Magnolia House.

Tensely she waited as the phone rang. But when his drawling baritone answered "Hello," she almost lost her nerve. "Hello?" he asked a second time, an edge of annoyance in his tone.

"This is Vicki," she forced herself to say. "And I've got a big problem down at the computer center," she added before he could draw any wrong conclusions.

Immediately he was all business. It was almost as if she were just another DDI employee and not the woman to whom he'd made passionate love the night before. And under the circumstances, Vicki was grateful for his impersonal demeanor. She didn't want to call up any heartbreaking images from the night before. From now on things would be strictly impersonal between her and Clay, she vowed.

"Why don't you tell me about it," he suggested.

Quickly Vicki filled him in on the details.

"I'll talk to the operator and call you back," he promised.

Almost before Vicki could hang up the phone, she saw the operator responding to Clay's call in the computer room. Clay must have been frank and to the point because not more than a minute later the diffident young man was sauntering in her direction.

"I see you've got some pull," he commented sarcastically as he leaned in the door of her office.

"Does that mean I can use the system?" she shot back, no longer able to keep the edge of antagonism out of her voice.

"Suit yourself."

Vicki watched as he began to reload the tapes to restart his accounting program. Whatever he thought, she really didn't want to crash the system again. This time she'd have to be more careful. The first thing to do was to determine whether the problem was in her work station or the main computer. Picking up the key to the remote facility down the hall, Vicki grabbed her documentation and headed out the door.

But once she began to try retrieving from the main computer again, the results were equally disastrous, and she knew what kind of greeting she'd receive in the computer room. Unfortunately, the operator's reaction lived up to her worst expectations. When she came down the hall to apologize, she wasn't allowed to say a word in her defense.

"I knew what was going to happen if you started messing around again," he raged. "But Harper wouldn't listen to a lowly operator. Maybe you'd like to run this accounting program yourself."

"How about if I run it?" a harsh voice cut in.

Both she and the computer operator turned to her left. They had been so intent on their confrontation that neither had noticed the arrival of C. L. Harper.

"She crashed the system again," the operator announced as if that explained everything. Then with an angry shift of his shoulders, he added, "I've had it. If you want to run the system, then go ahead." And with that he turned on his heels and headed toward the door with more energy than she'd seen him exhibit all afternoon.

"Wait a minute. I won't take this kind of insubordination," Clay shouted at his back. But the young man didn't seem to value his job very much because he didn't even break stride.

"I'm sorry you had to deal with someone like that," Clay apologized in a serious voice. Then a strange expression played across his rakish features before bringing a spark of amusement to his blue eyes. "But I wish he'd stayed around a little longer," he confided.

"Why? Are you a masochist?" Vicki couldn't help asking.

Clay shook his head ruefully. "Well, I tried calling Smith before I came, but I didn't get an answer. The problem is," he added with a sheepish grin, "I don't know how to run the system."

Despite her present grim circumstances, the fact that the golden boy of the computer industry didn't know how to operate his own computer system struck Vicki so funny that she couldn't repress a giggle. She tried to choke the slightly hysterical reaction back, but the more she thought about it, the more outrageous it became. And soon tears were streaming down her cheeks and her side hurt from laughing.

Clay watched her with faint surprise, as though he were somewhat knocked off balance by her amusement. Had he thought she would be so crushed by his rejection that she would be unable to function? Vicki wondered fleetingly. Well, she wasn't going to give him that satisfaction.

Finally he replied with mock indignation. "Vice-presidents of multi-million-dollar corporations are far too busy making important management decisions," he began in a voice thick with feigned pomposity, "to have time for experimenting with operating systems."

Vicki gave him an assessing look as she accepted the handkerchief Clay offered to wipe her eyes. She was determined now not to let him know how much he had hurt her. She might have made a fool of herself, but she had some pride left. What's more, time was pressing. She had no choice but to get the conversation back on a serious track.

"I hope we can figure it out together, then," she told him. "Because if we don't, the whole Montgomery demonstration is down the drain tomorrow."

Clay responded to her businesslike tone immediately. "Why don't you fill me in on exactly what's been happening?"

Briefly Vicki described her recent test in detail. As she talked, Clay's expression sobered. Occasionally he jotted down a few notes or interrupted with a perceptive question that helped Vicki clarify the problem in her own mind.

"The first thing we've got to do is figure out how to reboot the main computer," Clay pointed out as they headed back toward the console. "The manuals ought to be around here somewhere."

A quick search of the console desk produced the instructions for restarting the computer. But like all too many computer guides, they must have been written for someone who already knew the fundamentals of operating DDI's equipment. Even with the book it took more than half an hour of trial and error before they finally got the system up.

"I'm going to have them start rewriting this documentation first thing tomorrow," Clay mumbled to himself as the printer began to spew out successful load messages at last.

"I'll second that," Vicki agreed.

"Listen, why don't I stay here with the system while you run your test again," Clay suggested.

She gave him a thankful look and then returned to her office. Glancing at her watch, she was shocked to see how late it was. Time seemed to be racing past like an Olympic runner. Only she was the one who was going to lose the race if the problem didn't clear up soon.

As she began to go through the drill again, there was a

deep frown on her face. It was all happening again. And somewhere in the back of Vicki's mind a nagging doubt was beginning to grow about the coincidence of this problem happening now. Should she voice that doubt to Clay? she debated. What good would that do now? It would only sound as though she were trying to wiggle out of the problem by assigning someone else the blame. That would get her nowhere. And besides, there was always the possibility that the problem really was in her system. Better to check out her own software as thoroughly as possible. Vicki's steps were heavy when she finally retraced her path to the computer room.

"You don't have to tell me, it happened again," Clay commiserated. "I've already started a system trace." But his words held little comfort.

Vicki shook her head dispiritedly. "There could be some little bug in the Montgomery software that's causing all this. And even if I had the whole staff on it, we'd never get it fixed by tomorrow."

Clay took her by the shoulders, his blue eyes fierce. "You're not a quitter, Vicki. And besides," he added trying to lighten her mood. "You've been around in the computer industry long enough to know that no one accepts the blame for problems until proven guilty—and often not even then. We're going to check this thing out in every possible way—even if we have to stay here all night."

Were Clay's thoughts taking the same turn hers had? Vicki wondered. But just then the noisy hum of the printer ceased, indicating that the system trace was complete. The thought was lost as Vicki followed Clay over to where the printout lay stacked neatly behind the equipment. Clay tore off their report and began studying the results closely. Vicki peered over his shoulder trying to decipher the analysis herself. Unfortunately, there wasn't enough information to isolate the problem, and Vicki's worried expression deepened.

"I knew this wasn't going to be easy," she groaned.

"We'll find it," Clay assured her confidently. "Don't worry."

Vicki wanted to believe him, but it became more and more difficult as they tried and exhausted leads. It was many hours before the tedious work yielded the important clue they needed.

"It looks like the problem may not be in your software after all," Clay observed, pointing to a series of communication tables provided by the trace.

"You could be right," Vicki muttered under her breath, remembering her earlier suspicions as she drew Clay's attention to a message at the bottom of the next page. "This says your system has the wrong equipment type configured for the work station on the output link. But how could that be possible? It worked okay yesterday."

Clay shook his head. An expression that she couldn't quite read crossed his lean features. "Seems strange to me too," he admitted. "But sometimes errors do creep in," he added, in a voice that somehow lacked real conviction.

Suddenly Vicki had an inspiration. "Why don't we try changing the internal communication table from the console and see if those error messages go away."

"You're pretty sharp. But you know that, don't you?" he said, shooting her an approving glance as he sat down in front of the console.

Vicki crossed her fingers for good luck as Clay keyed in the necessary changes. Like magic, the communication errors vanished, and with them all thoughts in Vicki's mind about how the errors originated in the first place. The only important thing was that the mess was cleared up now. Thank God, she thought to herself, as she let out the breath she'd been holding.

"I'll go try my test again," she told Clay.

This time it worked as though the problem had never existed. And suddenly the adrenaline that had been keeping Vicki going for so many hours seemed to ebb away, leaving her almost faint. Vicki returned to report her success. But when she tried to thank Clay for his help, he waved away her expression of gratitude.

"All in a day's work, and besides," he said with genuine admiration in his eyes, "you're the one who solved the problem." Then he added in a self-mocking tone of voice, "But I was the one who was smart enough to lure you down to Stone Mountain in the first place."

Vicki blushed and then looked down at her watch. "It's after midnight," she exclaimed.

"So it is," said Clay. "This happens to me all the time. When I get involved with a problem, I lose all sense of the hours passing. But you're not used to this kind of schedule, and you must have worked right through dinner."

It was true, Vicki realized, unable to keep from swaying slightly on her feet. "You're right. I could use something to eat. And after that, I'm going to collapse in bed. And you could use the same prescription," she recommended, taking in Clay's own disheveled appearance. His blue eyes were rimmed with red, his dark hair looked as though he had been raking his hands through it, and his knit sport shirt was rumpled.

Together they powered down the system and closed up shop. Fifteen minutes later, Clay and Vicki were settled in his sports car.

"At this time of night, the only place we can get anything to eat around here is the Burger Palace."

"Burgers and fries sound great," Vicki assured him, as her stomach grumbled in response.

They ate their fast food banquet in the parking lot of the restaurant, then they headed back toward Magnolia House. Vicki couldn't stay awake in the car on the way home. It seemed as if she had only closed her eyes for a moment when she felt Clay gently shake her.

"Where are your keys?" he questioned, getting out of the car and coming around to her side.

"Pocketbook," she managed to mumble as he helped her to her feet. It was wonderful to have Clay's warm, strong arm supporting her waist as he guided her toward the door of her room. And in response, she threw her own arm around his neck. She heard him fumbling with the lock. And then he was helping her across the room with the intent of settling her on the bed.

But Vicki was so somnolent that she didn't disengage her arm from around his neck. The effect was to pull him down on the bed with her.

"I take it this is an invitation," he drawled, brushing a light kiss along her brow line.

She didn't even hear the question.

Clay slipped her arm from around his neck and pulled her more comfortably against his body. He wanted to kiss her again, but from her even breathing he knew that she was already asleep.

He intended just to give himself the pleasure of holding her close for a few moments before he left, but he didn't realize the extent of his own fatigue. Within minutes he was sleeping as soundly as she.

10

~oooooooooo~

The insistent ringing of the phone dragged Vicki back to consciousness. Sleepily, she tried to reach for it, but a blue-jean clad male leg restrained her.

My God, Clay Harper was in her bed again! The last thing she could remember clearly was having something to eat at a drive-in. After that everything was a blur of exhaustion. What had happened after he'd brought her home?

The six-foot computer whiz beside her was beginning to come to life himself. With a little twisting, Vicki was able to slip out from under him and answer the phone.

"This is your wake-up call," a female voice chirped.

"Oh, uh, thank you," Vicki said, pushing a lock of auburn hair out of her face and rubbing the sleep from her eyes.

Turning back to the bed, she took in Clay's grinning countenance. His thick hair was tousled, and his lean cheeks roughened by a day's growth of dark beard. But he was still heartbreakingly handsome.

"I guess I must have fallen asleep. Did anything interesting happen after that?" he quipped.

His question took her off guard, and she felt herself blush. But a quick inspection told her that they were both fully dressed. Sleeping together last night had undoubtedly been no more than just that—sleeping.

Instead of answering Clay's impertinent query, Vicki heaved a pillow in his direction. But he rolled aside and pulled her back down against him on the bed. "Was that a yes or a no?" he whispered seductively into her ear, holding her captive in his warm embrace.

Despite her annoyance at his teasing attitude, Vicki had to admit that it felt good to snuggle in Clay's arms. However, when his lips found hers, she didn't respond. It was true that she wanted nothing more than to stay there in his embrace without worrying about their complicated relationship. But that was impossible. This was the morning of the big demonstration.

"Clay, I have to get down to my office as soon as possible," she murmured, pushing gently but determinedly at his chest.

"I have to get ready, too," he said, his voice edged with regret. "But I just can't let you go. Not yet."

His lips found hers again, and despite herself, Vicki could not help giving herself over to the warm pleasure of it. After they had made love the night of the ball, she had felt compelled to share her feelings with him. And he had repeated his speech about "no commitments." That had hurt her deeply. And yet, when she really needed him yesterday, he had come through for her as few men would have. There was no reason why he should have spent hours helping her straighten out her trouble with the main computer—except his feelings for her. Maybe those feelings were stronger than he would admit. And maybe that meant there was hope for their relationship after all. His hands were on her back, stroking and pulling her closer. And she felt herself melting against the length of his body.

But before her thirst for him could be satisfied, she felt him push her gently away. "You're a sweet temptation before breakfast," he teased, running his fingers through her loosened hair and touching his lips to her temples. "But we do have to get up. Perhaps we can continue this uh, discussion, later."

"Clay! You're impossible," Vicki admonished.

"Yes, I know. But with a little encouragement, I might reform." Pulling Vicki to her feet, he gave her a playful pat on the behind. "I think we both ought to hit the showers."

"You in your room and me in mine," Vicki told him firmly.

"Party pooper," Clay returned lightly. But he was already heading for the door.

After Vicki had shed last night's wrinkled clothing and adjusted the temperature of her own shower, she stepped under the warm spray and let the soothing water revive her. For a few moments she had time to think about Clay Harper.

Again she dwelled on the way he had gone all out for her last night. That thought did more to lift Vicki's spirits than if he had presented her with a bouquet of flowers. Clay must care! And her next challenge would be to make him realize it.

With a renewed sense of purpose, Vicki stepped out of the shower and began to towel herself dry. No jeans today. This was a VIP demonstration. Instead of her usual casual attire, she selected a black linen suit, a contrasting print blouse, and elegant black pumps. The ensemble made her look like an executive, she decided, as she gave herself a last inspection before picking up her briefcase and heading out the door. On her way to the DDI building, she checked the printed agenda for the day. Every minute was accounted for, starting with a continental breakfast in the DDI conference facility.

When she reached the oak-paneled room, Clay was already surrounded by a group of obviously important visitors. Gail, looking neat and professional in a beige suit, was busy playing hostess, but managed a sincere "good luck" as she handed Vicki a cup of coffee. After she had a few sips of the steaming, revitalizing liquid and a bite of a luscious peach Danish, Clay managed to catch her attention and motioned her to join him.

"Vicki, I'd like you to meet the chairman of our board, Ned Whitney, and some of our other top executives," he explained, making the introductions.

She went through the motions of polite conversation, but her attention was focused on the dynamic vice-president beside her. The expensive cut of the conservative pin-striped suit he wore served only to emphasize his powerful masculinity. For Vicki, he was by far the most attractive man in the room. And his command of the situation was evident by the way the visiting dignitaries responded to him. No one would suspect, she mused, how C. L. Harper had spent the night before. He looked too alert and in control to have spent the night sleeping in his clothes in someone else's bed. Vicki hid a secret smile as she felt her cheeks begin to glow. She certainly wasn't going to tell on him—considering that it had been her bed. But she had more important things to be concerned about, she reminded herself as she mentally reviewed her own demonstration only a few minutes away.

At that moment Martin Loomis, coffee and Danish in hand, joined their group and was introduced around. He seemed confident and in good spirits. But when Clay unconsciously touched her shoulder as he mentioned a special feature of Montgomery's work station, she saw her rival give the two of them a speculative look from under hooded lashes.

Was he just reacting to the extra plug for Montgomery, or had he seen Clay leave her room this morning? she wondered, suddenly uneasy. After all, no matter what her feeling for Clay, there were all sorts of ways their relationship could be misconstrued—especially by her rival for the big word processing contract. Vicki repressed a shiver.

The harm was already done, and there was little she could do to correct Loomis's wrong impressions even if he had them. She'd just have to go on the assumption that everything was okay. Besides, she remembered one of Barry's favorite sayings: "If it's not broke—don't fix it!" The thought brought a glimmer of a smile to her face.

"Feeling confident about the test?" Loomis purred. There was the slightest hint of satisfaction in his tone, as if he knew something Vicki didn't. But before she could react, Clay was clearing his throat.

"As you've seen from your agenda," he began, "we've a marathon of activities planned for today. So I'd like to get started right now. First stop today is a state-of-the-art demonstration of office automation. DDI is currently evaluating two promising proposals for fully computerizing all executive and office-related activities. We've started with two prototype configurations in this building set up by Ms. Johnson, from Montgomery Systems, and Mr. Loomis, representing Prentice Systems, who will be conducting this morning's demonstrations. As you know, one of their companies will be selected to complete phase two of our plans—installing similar equipment in convenient locations throughout Stone Mountain Center so that residents will be able to communicate with DDI computer resources right from their homes."

His speech was smoothly delivered as he led the group of VIPs down the hall into the special office-of-the-future terminal room that had been set up for this purpose. A few moments passed while the high-powered guests took time to inspect the area. Then Clay turned to Martin Loomis. "Why don't you go first?" he suggested.

"With pleasure," Vicki's competitor agreed.

She and the rest of the group watched as Loomis put his equipment through its paces. This was the first time she'd seen a demo of his system, and Vicki was dismayed to realize how competitive it was. Loomis kept showing how easy the equipment was to use—even for people who had never been near a computer.

"You've really invested a lot of effort in making your system 'user friendly,'" the DDI board chairman commented, "and it looks like it's paid off."

Vicki could see her rival basking in the compliment. If she were honest, she'd have to admit there wasn't that much difference in the two systems. Both had easy-to-use word processing capabilities, quick information retrieval features, and electronic mail. The only extras that Montgomery had were the sophisticated built-in spelling dictionary and the executive calendar.

If the flurry of questions that followed his demonstration were any indication, then the Prentice system was given top marks. Martin Loomis was going to be a hard act to follow. Vicki found herself glancing over at Clay for reassurance. His blue eyes met hers with a look that said, "I know you can do it."

I hope everything's still functioning, Vicki prayed, as she sat down at her own work station. But she and Clay had done their utmost yesterday to set things right, and she'd just have to assume the best.

Vicki took a deep breath and began her introduction to the Montgomery system in a voice that did not betray the flutter of nerves in her stomach. Out of the corner of her eye, she could see Martin Loomis watching her intently. He was probably as interested in assessing his competition as she had been, Vicki told herself, trying to ignore the feel of his eyes on the back of her neck. Without missing a beat, she began creating office correspondence and showing how it could be transmitted to remote stations with the touch of a button.

"What about your file retrieval system?" one of the watching officials prompted.

Vicki felt herself tense again. It was during file retrieval that she'd run into problems yesterday, and she'd wanted to save that part for last, just in case the problem recurred. But now she would have to go ahead with it.

After setting the parameters, she glanced up briefly and happened to catch a peculiar expression on Loomis's face. It almost looked as if he were as tense as she. Was it because he knew about the difficulties she'd been having? she asked herself fleetingly. But then her attention returned to the display. The requested data was being accessed without a flaw. And Vicki slowly let out the breath she hadn't known she was holding.

Loomis's eyes flickered from her screen across to the main computer room and back as if he couldn't believe what had happened. Vicki saw him open his mouth and then close it quickly without saying anything. But she was too relieved by her success to pay much attention to the opposition now.

The flurry of questions that followed her prepared demonstration kept her busy for the next half-hour. When she finally looked up, she spotted her rival and Clay huddled in the corner, conferring heatedly. Noting that the questions were over, Clay detached himself and addressed the group again.

"I think a break might be in order now. There's coffee and Danish down the hall. Why don't you relax for a few minutes, and then we'll go on with the tour."

After Gail had escorted the VIPs out of the room, Martin Loomis, his face red with barely suppressed fury, turned accusingly to Vicki.

"I've let it go till now, but I want it on record that if you win this contract, I'll fight it every inch of the way," he snarled.

"What, what are you talking about?"

"I think you know," Loomis sneered, an ugly expression on his face.

"Just a second," Clay interjected.

But her rival was not about to be derailed. "If Ms. Johnson gets this contract, it will be through unfair advantage," he insisted.

Vicki shook her head. What he was saying just didn't make any sense. And then all of the sudden it did. Her heart beat wildly as she remembered his peculiar expression when her file retrieval test worked like a charm. Sabotage! If Martin had been responsible for that bug in the system, he'd be mad as hell when his little plan backfired. But for the moment she decided to keep these thoughts to herself.

"Do you deny that you've been sleeping with C. L. Harper in order to make sure your system would be picked over mine?" he jeered.

The blood drained from Vicki's face. So Loomis had seen her and Clay together after all.

"You're way out of line, Martin," Clay cautioned, his voice dangerously cold.

"I think the DDI top brass would like to know about your part in this little affair," Loomis shot back.

Vicki had had enough. She wasn't going to let Martin get away with that kind of accusation without letting him know what she suspected about him. "I think the VIPs would be most interested in your recent activities—"

But before she could say any more, Clay cut her off with a cold, icy look. "I suggest that you don't say anything you might regret later, Ms. Johnson."

Clay's angry expression was replaced by one that she couldn't quite read. And his next words confused her even more.

"Martin, I think we can settle this between the two of us, without involving Ms. Johnson," he began smoothly, his tone conciliatory.

That seemed to satisfy Loomis, and he shot her a triumphant look, as if he already had the contract in his pocket.

Clay turned to Vicki with a closed expression. "I think it would be wise for you to return to your room now. I'll be in touch with you later."

Vicki's jaw dropped open. Had she heard him right? Was he really sending her away? Was he going to work out some deal with Martin Loomis in order to keep him quiet? It seemed impossible. But how could she construe Clay's words in any other way? Suddenly she felt physically ill, as though a wrecking ball had punched her in the stomach. What a fool she'd been to trust Clay Harper. How could he have been so supportive the night before and then turn against her like this? Was he capitulating to Loomis to save his own neck? She didn't know what to think now. All she could do was turn pleading eyes to Clay. But he met her gaze coldly.

"I'll be in touch with you later," he repeated pointedly.

With as much dignity as she could muster, Vicki picked up her papers and fled the room.

11

~eeeeeeeeeee~

Tears welled up in Vicki's green eyes as she walked quickly up the path back to her room. She felt the career and the professional reputation that she'd worked so hard to build was in a shambles. What's more, her relationship with Clay seemed to have fallen to pieces as well. Loomis's charge that she'd been sleeping with Clay to win the contract was certainly untrue, but Vicki had to admit it might well look like that to an outsider, and there was no way she could defend herself against such a charge. Maybe it even looked that way to Clay. Maybe he thought she'd sold her body to him for a contract.

The thought unnerved her so much that fresh tears blinded her as she reached for the door and stumbled inside. Slumping against the wall and looking unhappily at the bed where she and Clay had lain, she pondered her predicament. How could the man who had been so tender the night before think so ill of her? But how else could she explain his peremptory dismissal? Even now he and Loomis might be sneering at her.

Vicki pulled herself up short. No, she was sure Clay wouldn't do that. But he had worked himself into a corner with her. Maybe he was feeling claustrophobic about their affair and was looking for an easy way out and Loomis's accusation had presented him with a convenient escape route. Vicki put her hand over her forehead and closed her eyes. She had to admit that made sense, but it didn't make her feel any better. And then there was the whole question of her job. What would she tell Ellen? How could she explain this mess to her boss? "Oh, Vicki," she said out loud, shaking her head despairingly, "don't you ever learn?" The Jerry Pratt incident had been bad enough, but this Clay Harper fiasco was a thousand times worse. Vicki wondered whether she would ever recover from it.

Just thinking about the way she was losing this contract made her stomach knot, and she began to gasp slightly from the tightness in her chest. Clenching her fists, she took a deep breath and tried to steady her nerves. "I can't stay on this emotional merry-go-round anymore," she announced to the empty room. "I need to clear my head. I've got to get out of here."

Decisively, she crossed the room and opened the wardrobe door. Pulling out her suitcases, she plopped them on the bed and undid their locks. In a few moments piles of hastily folded lingerie, slacks, blouses, and dresses filled the luggage. Looking around the denuded room, Vicki checked to see that she had packed everything. Then turning, she strode quickly to the bathroom to gather what remained in there.

But just as she went to scoop up the last of her makeup, she glanced in the mirror and stopped abruptly. There was no way she could face a crowd in the airport looking like she'd been dragged through Stone Mountain Lake. Her swollen, red-rimmed eyes and tear-stained cheeks would advertise that she'd just been through an emotional catastrophe. What's more, her hair was hang-

ing in lank strings around her wrecked features. Setting
down the makeup bottles with a clatter, she turned on
the cold water, dampened a washcloth, and held it up to
her face, letting the cool wetness soothe her aching eyes.
What do I do now? she asked herself grimly. Everything
was such a mess!

Maybe she needed to go back home and talk to Sally.
Her sister always seemed to be able to put things in
perspective. Perhaps she'd be able to work that major
miracle again this time, too. It was a threadbare hope, but
Vicki clung to it. When she took the cloth away, her face
looked somewhat restored. Briskly, she ran a brush
through her hair and dabbed on fresh makeup. Feeling a
bit better about her appearance, if nothing else, she
shoved her makeup into a soft plastic case and strode
back out into the room to put the finishing touches on the
packing.

When the last of her belongings were tucked away,
Vicki locked her suitcases with a decisive snap and
struggled to heave them off the bed. But just as she was
wrestling them across the rug, she was startled by a sharp
rap on the door. Vicki's eyes opened wide, and she gave
the closed barrier a stricken look. Dropping the heavy
luggage, she stood staring at it, not quite knowing what to
do. She didn't want to talk to whoever was out there. All
she wanted was to get out of here without being seen.
Maybe the intruder would go away if she didn't answer,
she told herself. She stood motionless as the second
impatient rap echoed through the thick wood, and her
heart thudded wildly as she remembered that the door
was unlocked. Maybe she could tiptoe up and turn the
key, she speculated, eyeing the metal bolt. But as she
started to inch forward, the door flew open, and Clay
Harper came storming into the room.

"What the hell are you doing? Why didn't you answer?" he demanded. His eyes narrowed to blue slits as
he took in the closed suitcases at Vicki's feet. Walking

over to the pile of luggage, he picked one of them up, feeling its weight. Then stalking over to the wardrobe and throwing open its doors, he stood with hands on his narrow hips, eyeing its empty depths. "I see what you're doing," he declared in a slow careful voice. "But I don't understand. Why in the world are you sneaking out?"

Vicki threw up her hands in a hopeless gesture and sank back down on the bed. "You know quite well why I'm leaving. There's nothing left here for me but humiliation. It's best that I go before it gets worse."

Running his hand through his hair in a gesture of impatience, Clay walked across the room and stood staring down at her. "I don't understand women at all," he said, shaking his head. "And maybe I never will. Here you've won the contract and you're taking off for parts unknown. It doesn't make any sense."

Vicki shot him an incredulous look. This was certainly the most confusing morning of her life. What in the world could Clay mean? "But how could I have won the contract?" she finally threw out. "What about Loomis's charges?"

He waved his hand with a dismissive gesture. "You know they're not true."

"That's right. But I didn't think you knew it, Clay."

His expression softened, and he sat down beside her on the bed. Taking her hand in his, he said firmly, "Of course, I know it." Then tilting her head toward him, he demanded, "Are you trying to make a getaway because I asked you to leave back there after the demonstration?"

Vicki nodded.

Clay sighed. "We never seem to understand each other, do we? And I suppose this time it's my fault. I wanted Loomis to confess, and I knew he wouldn't while you were there."

"Confess to what?" she asked, but Vicki knew the answer.

"You must have guessed by now, that it was Martin

Loomis who sabotaged your software," Clay stated baldly. "Were you aware that he hadn't shown up at the ball two nights ago?"

Vicki nodded in agreement. That was true, she reflected. At the beginning of the evening, she had noted her competitor's absence, but later she had become so wrapped up in the enchantment of being with Clay that she wouldn't have noticed a parade of elephants stomping around on the dance floor. The ridiculous image of waltzing pachyderms flittered through her imagination, and despite the seriousness of their conversation, she just had to smile.

Not noticing her expression, Clay continued. "While everyone was playing out a fantasy of the Old South, Loomis was tinkering with your computer software."

"How did you find out?" she wanted to know.

The corners of his mouth lifted in a wry grin. "I did a bit of sleuthing earlier today. I cornered Todd Provost of the operations staff and had a little chat. Seems that Loomis had wanted to put in some overtime two nights ago, but it was on the main computer, not his. And for a not-so-small fee, Provost allowed him to do so."

Vicki's brow began to wrinkle. So that's how it happened. While she'd been lying clasped in Clay's arms, swept away by passion, Loomis had been coldbloodedly tampering with Montgomery Systems' DDI computer interface tables. She clenched her fists as she contemplated the sheer audacity of the man.

Clay seemed equally irritated. Standing up, he took a few steps toward the other side of the room. Then turning to Vicki, he continued, "When I confronted Loomis with the fact a few minutes ago, he folded like an accordion and backed off from his charge against you right away. The man, it seems, is more interested in protecting his own reputation than in making trouble for you, Vicki." Clay sat back down on the bed and leaned back on his elbows. "Industrial sabotage is a crime, you know."

Vicki's eyes widened. "Do you intend to prosecute, Clay?"

The tall, dark computer genius shook his head. "No, at this point, it's more mess than it's worth. The important thing is that Montgomery Systems will get the contract fair and square, so there's no reason for you to be running out on me. I've seen enough to know that you do have the better system. Loomis's dirty tricks just pushed the decision up a few weeks." The fierce expression on Clay's face had softened as he said this, and he put his arm around her waist and pulled her toward him. His voice lowered to a caress. "We'll still have to work closely together to tie up all the loose ends." He slid his hand up the length of her arm and turned her body toward his.

For a moment, Vicki felt nothing but confusion as she tried to sort out the startling reversals of the last hour. Only minutes before, she'd been ready to flee Stone Mountain in defeat. Now Clay was handing her success on a silver platter. But that wasn't all he was handing her, she re lized, as his arm tightened on her back and he leaned closer. Clay wanted to make love to her again and had already begun the preliminary moves. And based on past performances, he had every reason to think she'd be willing.

Even as the thought ran through her mind, she found Clay was pressing her closer and exploring her lips with his. At the same time his hand pushed her shoulders gently down, maneuvering her to a horizontal position on the bed. Leaning over her, he deepened the kiss. While his fingers stroked the vulnerable flesh of her throat, he feathered little caresses on her chin. But as his fingers reached to the buttons of her blouse, Vicki lay passively in his embrace, thinking hard.

Always before she had let her emotions rule her head where Clay Harper was concerned, but this time, she vowed, she would protect herself. He still hadn't said anything about love and was still avoiding a commitment, and she wasn't going to let him get away with his seemingly ambivalent attitude toward their relationship. It would not be easy, she acknowledged. Clay always seemed able to kindle a flame within her, and this time was no exception. Already little waves of heat had begun to lick at her, and the urge to arch her body against him in feminine invitation burned inside her. But if she was ever going to get off this dangerous emotional rollercoaster, she'd better get herself in hand and look squarely at the cost of the ticket.

Using all her willpower, Vicki forced her aching body to stillness, and Clay's attentions suddenly became less ardent. Sensing her lack of response, he lifted his head and looked down at her questioningly. "What's wrong, Vicki?"

Her eyes met his without blinking. "Let me up, Clay. This time it isn't going to work."

His dark brows furrowed, and his blue eyes scrutinized her for a moment, taking in the closed expression on her face. Then he shifted abruptly away from her, and she was free from his weight. "What is it?" he asked again, a wary note in his voice now.

Very deliberately, Vicki sat up and straightened her blouse, using the time to think about what she would say. Flutters of anxiety had replaced the quivers of excitement that Clay's lovemaking had aroused, and she took a deep breath to try and quell them. It was now or never, she told herself. She loved Clay too much. She had to make him face what he was doing to his life—even if it meant losing him. Meeting Clay's gaze again, Vicki said, with all the calmness she could muster, "Clay, I've already told you that I love you. And that hasn't changed. But if it's going to remain one-sided, then I have no choice but to break our relationship off right now."

Having finally said the words that had been festering inside her, she felt a sudden sense of relief. They'd been bottled up for a long time, she realized. And now that they were out, she was glad she'd had the courage to say them—even if it meant that she and Clay were finished.

"I suppose you're talking about marriage." Clay set his mouth in a firm line and shook his head. "Vicki, all along I've been square with you. I've told you more about myself than I've told any other woman. I thought you understood. You know I'm just not the marrying type."

Well, there it was, Vicki thought, staring fixedly into his set countenance. Now she would have to come to terms with it. Either she was going to settle for an affair or she'd have to find the courage to call it off now. Folding her hands tightly in her lap, she continued to look directly at him. "Then I guess it's all over, Clay. I'm not going to accept anything less."

Under his tan, Clay went white. Momentarily he'd dropped his defensive mask, and Vicki could see that he was stunned by her uncompromising statement. Clearly he hadn't expected anything like that from her. "Knowing what we could have, you're willing to just walk away?" he rasped.

Vicki clenched her teeth. "I don't want just an affair. I want you. I want marriage and children and to know you'll be with me always. And," she added, lifting her head high, "if I can't have that, I'd rather have nothing at all." The stark words dropped into the silence like stones heaved into an echoing well. When the echoes died away there was another long, heavy silence.

"I see," Clay said, finally.

Vicki's voice was tight. "I'm not sure you do see. Maybe you should stop and take a look at what you're doing to your own life."

Without answering her, Clay stood up and went to the door. As his hand closed around the knob, he paused and turned back to her. "I've given you all my reasons. You can't honestly want to be married to a man like me.

I'm already married to my work," he bit out, "and I probably haven't many years left anyhow."

It was the same old song and dance, and though she knew he believed what he said, Vicki had lost patience with it now. Her redheaded temper was beginning to reach the point of no return. Rising from the bed, she marched up to the man who'd had such a cataclysmic effect on her.

Facing him squarely, she said, "Clay Harper, even if you were going to die next year, I'd still want that time with you. But I don't believe for a minute that you're anything but a healthy male specimen with a crazy hangup that you use as an excuse to keep people from getting too close." She clenched her small fists at her side and clipped out defiantly, "I've had enough of it. The Montgomery contract here can be handled just as well by someone else now, and I'm going back to California. And if you care anything about me, or yourself for that matter, you'll stop spouting all this nonsense and go see a doctor."

Clay's expression was thunderous. "Well, that says it all, doesn't it," he muttered between his teeth. Then turning back to the door, he strode out, flinging it shut with a bang behind him.

While she tried to fight back the tears that once again threatened to wash over her, Vicki stared at the place where he'd stood. Resignedly and with a sinking heart, she turned to pick up the heavy suitcases once again.

When Vicki returned to the Montgomery Systems' office in Santa Barbara with the good news about the contract, she found her popularity had increased a thousand fold. Ellen greeted the tidings of her success with jubilant plans and immediately sent out the next wave of technicians to extend the system at Stone Mountain. But when the company president asked Vicki if she'd like to accompany the new group, the younger woman shook her head.

"I need a break," Vicki told Ellen firmly. "It's been hectic, and I'd like a slower pace for a while." Then she softened her refusal with a smile and added, "What's more I've missed being here."

Vicki was crushingly aware that it would take time to get over her disastrous affair with Clay. But she'd do it, she told herself. Even though the wound was now fresh and excruciatingly painful, it would heal eventually, and she would go on with her life. But for the time being, her raw emotions needed special treatment, and she attempted to anesthetize them by throwing herself into a whirl of activity. At work she plunged immediately into a new project for an industrial client. And her free time was spent with Sally. As before, she was taking her troubles to her big sister.

"I've never seen you so low," Sally commented one afternoon as the two young women sat by the pool watching Beth and Matthew splash in the shallows.

Vicki looked thoughtfully at the jacaranda tree in its spring flowering and tried to avoid acknowledging Sally's probing comment. But her sister was too sharp to be evaded in that way.

"Come on. Out with it," Sally insisted. "I know something's wrong. Is it a man?"

Vicki sighed and then grimaced ruefully. She was reluctant to talk about Clay. But deep down she knew that a frank conversation with Sally about the ill-fated love affair with Clay was inevitable. When she finally broke down and began to confide in her sister, she found that letting it all out did make her feel a little better.

As Vicki described the ups and downs of her involvement with Clay, Sally listened calmly. And when Vicki was through, her older sister reached out and put a comforting hand on her shoulder.

"Oh, honey, you have had it rough," she sympathized. "The guy sounds like a class A jerk. I'd like to give him a piece of my mind!"

Though Vicki was touched by Sally's protective attitude, she shook her head in contradiction. "He's not a jerk, Sal. He's everything I ever wanted in a man and more." Unable to meet her sister's eyes, Vicki bit her lip and looked down at her tightly folded hands. "He just didn't fall in love with me the way I did with him. I guess he can't be blamed for that."

Sally arched an impatient eyebrow. "Then he must be crazy. But in any case, you have to get over him and go on with your life."

Vicki knew her sister's advice was true. But how could she take it? At this moment, getting on with a life that didn't include Clay seemed purposeless.

But Sally was determined to drag her sister out of her depression. "I've got a great idea," she offered. "Why don't you take the bonus Ellen gave you and use it to redecorate that drab apartment of yours. If you want, I'll help you pick out wallpaper and paint. It'll be fun! We can go out to Five Points tomorrow and get started."

Vicki gave her sister a doubtful look. How could wallpaper and paint make her forget Clay? But maybe it was worth a try. Anything was better than the well of misery she found herself in now.

Two weeks later she was dipping into a bucket of wallpaper paste in her small kitchen when the doorbell chimed. Reluctantly setting down a sticky piece of the yellow print wallpaper she and Sally had chosen for its cheering qualities, Vicki wiped her paste-spattered hands on the old pair of blue jeans she had donned and picked her way through the rolls of paper and cans of paint to the door.

Before she opened it, she tugged at her sweatshirt and tucked a straggling bit of hair under her red bandana kerchief. But all thoughts of making herself more present-able flew away when she pulled the door open. She gasped and her hand shot to her mouth. A grinning Clay Harper stood in the doorway. His boyish smile widened as he took in her ragtag outfit. Then peering past her shoulder, he studied the disarray on her living room floor.

"Looks like you plan to stay here for a while," he said with a mischievous wink. "And that's bad news as far as I'm concerned. I was hoping to talk you into moving in with me." Brushing past her, he strolled casually beyond her bewildered figure and held up a roll of wallpaper. "Not bad. I could live with this if I had to."

Vicki's mouth parted in astonishment as she gaped at the tall, dark man who'd first intruded on her life only three months ago and who had since that time made total hash of her emotions. She thought she'd put him behind her, but here he was again, now calmly invading her private domain without so much as a by-your-leave. Collecting her scattered wits, she rushed forward and snatched the paper from his hand.

"Well, you won't have to live with it," she snapped, referring to his earlier remark. "We settled all this two weeks ago." She shot him a challenging look. "And I have no intention of moving in with you and being your mistress."

Clay gazed down at her, his blue eyes suddenly serious. "As I recall that conversation, you said you'd consider marriage."

"Marriage?" she repeated, inhaling sharply. Then taking a step backward, she added, "What do you mean by that?"

Wending his way across the untidy room, Clay cleared the couch of the pictures she'd temporarily taken from the wall and sat down. Motioning Vicki over, he patted the cushion next to him.

But Vicki stayed put and eyed her uninvited guest warily. What was this all about?

Suddenly he grinned. His darkly handsome face filled with charm, and Vicki felt all her defenses slip away. "I can't propose with you standing way over there across the room," he growled playfully. "Come sit next to me so I can talk to you."

Vicki's heart skipped a beat, and her legs began to feel rubbery. "Okay," she agreed at last. Guardedly, she made her way to where Clay waited.

As she settled herself primly at the opposite end of the couch, Clay studied her defensive posture wryly. Then abruptly reaching for her, he seized Vicki by the waist and hauled her across the expanse between them so that she found herself curled intimately in his arms.

"Hey, stop that!" she protested wriggling to escape.

But Clay only tightened his grip. His voice, when he spoke, was dead serious. "Vicki, I love you."

The words wove around her like a magical net. Immediately, she stopped struggling and peered up quizzically.

"I love you," he repeated, taking her face in his hand and tilting it toward him. His blue gaze melted into her green one. "I guess I've known that for a long time now, but I've been too stubborn to admit it."

Vicki felt as if all the breath had been knocked out of her. "Oh, Clay," she murmured brokenly. "Do you really mean what you're saying?"

For an answer, Clay bent his head and kissed her tenderly, his lips exploring hers with infinite softness. "Let's get married," he whispered. "I want you to be my wife."

He pulled back from her, but his hand remained on her head, fingering the kerchief and stroking the wisps of red-gold hair that had escaped around her forehead. "I'm not much of a bargain as a husband, but I love you very much, and I want you to be the mother of my children."

Vicki reacted with more astonishment, her green eyes stretching wide. "Children? But what about your feelings about commitment . . . your health—"

Clay cut into her garbled doubts. "You were right all along. I finally went to see a cardiologist," he admitted sheepishly. "You don't know how many times I picked up the phone to make an appointment and then slammed it down again. But I wasn't just afraid for myself anymore." He paused, giving her a level look. "There was a lot more riding on finding out the truth about myself because now there wasn't just me to consider. There was you. I knew that if he didn't give me a clean bill of health, I couldn't call you. I was never so frightened before in my life."

"Oh, Clay," Vicki murmured, wrapping her arms tightly around his waist. "I told you I wanted you—no matter what."

Clay touched her cheek tenderly with the side of his hand. "It doesn't matter now, Vicki. The man told me that with my heart I could give Methuselah a run for his money. That is, if everything else holds out." He looked down at his hands, which were now clasping Vicki's. "I've done a lot of thinking, and I realize that there are no guarantees in life. You just have to do the best you can. And for me, Vicki, you're the best. However long I've got, I want to spend that time with you."

A warm glow began to spread through Vicki's body. It was like a fairy tale come true. Her heart swelled with happiness. "Oh, Clay, of course I'll marry you. I've been so miserable without you the past two weeks. I even launched into this great project to get you off my mind," she said, gesturing at the shambles that was now her apartment.

Clay gave the torn-apart room a rueful look. "I suppose I'm going to have to help you get it back together before we can make plans to find our own place." The words were like a sweet promise.

"Yes, I guess it would be hard to rent in this condition," Vicki said with a breathless laugh.

"Does the bedroom look like this too?" Clay asked, his blue eyes glinting wickedly.

Vicki shook her head. "No, I hadn't gotten to that yet."

Clay was suddenly all business. "Good. Let's take a look in there and see what we need to do," he responded. In the next moment he had risen and was pulling her up by the hand. He looked around to the doorways leading off the living area. "Which one?" he demanded.

"The one on the left."

The words were no sooner out of Vicki's mouth when she found herself swept up in Clay's strong arms. And in the next instant he was striding recklessly across the littered floor.

"I do declare," she trilled, as he carried her past the picture window. "What will the neighbors think?"

Clay smiled down into her face and dropped a light kiss on her mouth. "Frankly, my dear," he said in his best deep Southern drawl, "I don't give a damn."

"Nor do I," Vicki agreed as Clay kicked open the door and walked to the bed. Settling her gently on the mound of embroidered, lacy boudoir pillows that were her weakness, he looked around at the luxuriously feminine room with its pale blue canopied bed and wicker furniture. "I don't think this needs much work at all. Why don't we start another project, instead?" he suggested with mock seriousness, as he bent to release her hair from its kerchief. When the bright tresses were spread out in a halo, he leaned down and placed his hands on either side of Vicki's head.

"Ever since you left, I've been dreaming of this. I haven't had a good night's sleep in days. Let me take your clothes off, darling, and look at your beautiful body."

There was a lump in Vicki's throat and tears of joy in her emerald eyes as Clay gently pulled off her sweatshirt, unzipped her jeans and pushed them down over her slender legs. When she was wearing only her beige lace bra and wispy, bikini panties, he knelt beside the bed and gently kissed the soft mounds of flesh that rose above the cups of her bra. Vicki quivered with delight at his sensuous touch. She reached in front to unhook the intrusive garment, but Clay laid his hand on hers.

"No, don't," he murmured. "Let me." As he undid the fastening and released her breasts from their confinement, his eyes seemed to burn over her body. Clay's warm hands began to stroke her curvaceous roundness. Her breasts swelled at his touch, and when he bent his head to circle an aroused nipple with his tongue, she moaned.

"Umm, I like this project," he said huskily, as Vicki arched her back to give him better access. Her slender fingers reached up to undo the buttons on his crisp tan sport shirt. As she worked on them, he helped by unfastening those on his sleeves. Then in a fluid motion, he pulled his shirt from his waistband, shrugged out of it, and dropped the unwanted garment on the floor.

Vicki's eyes strayed lovingly over his hard, muscled chest, anticipating the feel of it against her. But instead of moving toward her, Clay reached to unbuckle his belt. Soon his pants had joined the shirt on the floor, and he stood naked before her. Once again Vicki admired his magnificent body. He was beautiful, she thought, as she ached with the desire to feel his weight pressing her into the mattress.

"Clay, please . . ." she pleaded.

"Just let me look at you a moment," he answered in a thickened voice.

As Clay's scorching gaze dwelled on her, she felt herself wriggling in involuntary invitation. "Clay?" she whispered hoarsely.

And this time he responded to her plea, sinking with a groan on the bed beside her. He kissed her with barely restrained passion, his hands beginning once more to explore her womanly body. His touch ran lightly down the length of her bare arm and then stroked her breasts before moving down to her stomach—and then lower. Deftly, his fingers slipped beneath the elastic of her panties, and Vicki's arms tightened around his shoulders and she buried her face in his neck. The gesture seemed to enflame him even more. Pulling slightly away, he roughly slid her remaining garment off.

"God, Vicki," he groaned, "I want you so much!"

"Oh, Clay, I want you too," she whispered, her tongue teasing the bronze flesh of his neck.

The tantalizing sensation was too much for Clay. In one lithe movement, his body was on top of hers, and his knee was parting her yielding thighs.

"Are you ready for me, my darling?" he asked. "I can't wait any longer for you."

"I want you now."

In the next moment he was hers, entering her body with strong possession and seeming to unite with her completely. As she and Clay began to move together in rhythmic harmony, Vicki felt their beings meld into one. But by losing themselves, they gained something much greater. As they strove for a crescendo of mutual pleasure, they seemed to find a new identity rising from their fevered lovemaking. For both of them there was a yielding and giving, pushing them higher and higher toward an exhilarating peak of ecstasy.

"Oh, Clay," Vicki cried in the moment of her lyrical release. His hands tightened on her shoulders as he too found his own rapture. And then slowly they seemed to settle back to earth.

For a moment Clay's damp body rested on hers. And then he lifted his head and looked deeply into her eyes.

"I love you so much," he murmured tenderly. "I feel

so filled with love for you now that I have no room for anything else."

Vicki stared up at him mutely, but her gleaming eyes spoke volumes. There was so much to say, but now they would have a lifetime to communicate the depths of their love.

Finally, she smiled and returned teasingly, "Not even lunch?"

Clay cocked a dark eyebrow and the corner of his mouth lifted. "Well, now that you mention it . . ."

Looking him over with a wry smile, Vicki said, "Ah, you're dressed just perfectly for a picnic in bed."

Clay grinned.

"And," she added, "I just happen to have a few goodies for a picnic lunch in my refrigerator." She gestured airily around the room. "Since the setting is just right and we're both undressed for the occasion, why don't we take the afternoon off. You've been working hard, after all, and you need to have a little fun for a change."

Simultaneously they burst into laughter, collapsing against each other.

"Our life together will obviously be one big picnic," Clay assured his lover as they scrambled off the mattress.

"And as long as we stay in bed," Vicki assured him sagely, "there won't be any ants."

Clay grinned. Then putting his arm around her shoulder, he kissed her lightly on the forehead. "Oh, Vicki. I'm lucky to have you," he said, pulling her close and nuzzling her ear. "I can't believe, after all my crazy hangups and speeches about marriage, that you'd agree to be my wife."

"You are a lucky man," Vicki agreed with a teasing laugh. "Other women might have given up on you." Then sighing, she looked up into his blue eyes and gave him a playful smile. "I guess," she drawled, "I'm just susceptible to your brand of Southern persuasion."

Silhouette Desire
15-Day Trial Offer

*A new romance series
that explores
contemporary relationships
in exciting detail*

Six Silhouette Desire romances, free for 15 days!
We'll send you six new Silhouette Desire romances
to look over for 15 days, absolutely free! If you
decide not to keep the books, return them and owe
nothing.

**6 NEW SILHOUETTE DESIRE NOVELS DELIVERED
RIGHT TO YOUR HOME EACH MONTH**

 Silhouette Desire

**Silhouette Desire
320 Steelcase Rd. E., Markham,
Ontario L3R 2M1**

Please send me 6 Silhouette Desire romances to keep for 15
days absolutely free. If I like Silhouette Desire romances I
will return my payment with the invoice. I understand I will
receive 6 New Silhouette Desire novels delivered to my home
each month as soon as they are off the press, before they are
available in the stores. There are no additional postage,
handling or other hidden charges and you will bill me for 6
books at $1.95 each (Total $11.70) each month. A savings
off retail of 30 cents per book (total savings $1.80 per ship-
ment). There is no minimum number of books I must purchase
and I am free to cancel this arrangement at any time.

Name_____

Address_____

City_____ Prov._____

Postal Code_____ Tel. No. _____

Signature_____

(If under 18 Parent or Guardian must sign)

*This offer limited to one per household, expires March 31,
1984. If price increases are necessary you will be notified. We
reserve the right to grant membership.*

56BPA83B

INTRODUCING

Silhouette Intimate Moments

Romance books that will take you into the
private world of your desires and beyond.

15 DAY FREE TRIAL OFFER

We're introducing the newest, most exciting romance series
ever ... books so full of passion you won't be able to put them
down!

CONTEMPORARY SETTINGS, MODERN ROMANCE ...
The Silhouette Intimate Moments series was created for a
special kind of woman — one who isn't afraid to be swept away
by passion and adventure. Each book is 256 pages long ... filled
with dynamic, powerful characters ... and exotic, unusual
locales. These stories will capture your imagination ... you'll
feel as if they're happening to you!

THRILL TO 4 Books every month ...
If you think you're this kind of woman, you'll want to
experience Silhouette Intimate Moments. Just mail the attached
coupon, and we'll send you 4 books to preview for 15 days.

FREE 15 DAY TRIAL
When your books arrive, look them over for 15 days FREE.
If not delighted, simply return them and owe nothing. If you
wish to keep them, just pay the enclosed invoice. Then you'll
receive 4 new books every month as long as you're a subscriber.

4 BOOKS EACH MONTH
DELIVERED RIGHT TO YOUR HOME!
We'll send your books right to your home, as soon as they're
published. And this service is absolutely free — we pay all
postage, handling, packaging and other costs. You never have to
worry about missed titles or bookstore sell-outs!

1M583

GET READY TO BE SWEPT AWAY BY FANTASY AND
PASSION LARGER THAN LIFE
WITH

Silhouette Intimate Moments

SILHOUETTE INTIMATE MOMENTS MAY NOT BE
FOR EVERYONE, BUT THEY ARE FOR READERS
WHO WANT A MORE SENSUAL, CONTEMPORARY
ROMANCE.

Silhouette Intimate Moments

MAIL THIS COUPON TODAY TO

SILHOUETTE BOOK CLUB OF CANADA
320 STEELCASE RD. E., MARKHAM, ONTARIO L3R 2M1

YES! Please send me 4 Silhouette Intimate Moments novels
to preview for 15 days. If I am not delighted I can return
them and owe absolutely nothing! If I decide to keep them, I
will pay the enclosed invoice. Each book costs $2.25 (a total
of $9.00) with no postage, handling, or any other hidden
charges. A savings off retail of .25¢ per book (total savings
1.00 per shipment). I understand there is no minimum
number of books I must buy, and I can cancel this
arrangement at any time.

Name _____

Addres _____ Apt. # _____

City _____ Prov. _____

Postal Code _____ Tel. No. (   ) _____

Signature _____
(If under 18, parent or guardian must sign)

*This offer limited to one per household. Expires March 31, 1984. If price
increases are necessary, you will be notified.*

We reserve the right to grant membership

1M583